I0687605

Wild Wedding Weekend

by

Debra St. John

Wild Wedding Weekend

Contact Information:
info@thewildrosepress.com

Cover Art by *Angela Anderson*

The Wild Rose Press
PO Box 708
Adams Basin, NY 14410-0706
Visit us at www.thewildrosepress.com

Publishing History
First Champagne Rose Edition, 2010
Print ISBN 1-60154-699-8

Published in the United States of America

"I really am sorry." Abby's mind whirled. Her thoughts tangled. The Noah she'd spent the last couple of days with wasn't anything like the man she'd imagined him to be. The man he'd claimed to be. Who was the real Noah?

She didn't have time to ponder the question, because he took both her hands in his, drawing her attention back to him. "Know this. While we're married. For this week, this trip, this asinine show, I am committed to you." He paused and raised one hand to tuck a wisp of hair behind her ear. "Totally. Completely. Committed. To you." With each word his voice and head lowered, until the last was a whisper against her lips.

Noah's hand slid around to the back of her neck, then up into her hair, unfastening the clip and tossing it aside. He tangled his fingers in the strands that fell free and held her close as he deepened the kiss.

Abby wrapped her arms around him as the tip of his tongue teased the fullness of her bottom lip. When she opened to him and he dipped inside, she almost melted from the flood of liquid heat that suffused her body. Warmth spread to her limbs and made her pliant as, his mouth never leaving hers, Noah lowered them both to the bed.

Praise for *WILD WEDDING WEEKEND**

"Debra St. John's *WILD WEDDING WEEKEND* is a fun, incredibly sexy and wildly romantic adventure you don't want to miss."
~*June Sproat, author of **Ordinary Me***

*Winner of the 2006 "Melody of Love" contest

~

What people are saying about Debra St. John...

THIS TIME FOR ALWAYS by Debra St. John**

"Ms. Debra St. John has created a magnificent storyline in this, her first published work...Her couple faced so many devastating situations that it was impossible to not get sincerely involved in their ups and downs...The sensual scenes were beautifully written...I highly recommend this book to anyone who enjoys an expressive romance with a happily ever after."
~*Brenda, reviewer for The Romance Studio (rated Five Hearts)*
"An excellent combination of romance, love, hope, family values with a gut-wrenching narrative..."
~*Bluebell, reviewer for Long and Short Reviews (rated Four Books)*

**TWRP Champagne Rose and Rosebud #1 Bestseller!
**A WRDF "Top Read"!
**Reader's Pick of the Month (November) at Jeannette Green Blogspot

Dedication

For my husband, John, who never fails to
encourage, support, and inspire me.
To my family, for your enthusiasm and excitement.
And to my friends,
thanks for being my sisters and brothers and
sharing your families with me.

Dear Reader,

I'm so thrilled you picked up a copy of *Wild Wedding Weekend*. This was a fun story to write, and I hope you enjoy the romance of Noah and Abby's adventure as much as I do. The mismatched, sometimes reluctant, couple learn many things about each other and themselves on their journey toward true love.

I always find it fun to write about places I've actually been to, so for Abby and Noah's honeymoon, they visit some of the same places my husband and I did on our honeymoon eleven years ago.

Happy Reading!

All the best,

Debra St. John
www.debrastjohnromance.com

Chapter One

"I can't believe I let you talk me into this."

Abby Walker paced around a tangle of backstage wires, props, and technicians. Ignoring the commotion around her, she listened to the voice of her longtime friend coming from the cell phone tucked against her ear.

"Oh, come on, Abby. It'll be fun," Claire wheedled.

"Fun? You call humiliating myself in front of a live studio audience fun? And with some guy I barely know."

"It won't be that bad, I promise. Besides, you know Noah."

"I've met the man three times. I'd hardly call that knowing him."

"He's out of town a lot. Travels for his job. It's not my fault." She sounded almost desperate.

"I know, I know. I don't think this will work. They'll find out I'm not you, and then we'll all be in trouble." She chewed a fingernail.

"Just give them your name. I'm sure they won't care, as long as they have a warm body for filming. And if you win—"

Did Claire sound almost hopeful?

"We'll just change the names back. Easy."

"If we win?" Abby asked. "Um, Claire, I don't think that's going to happen."

"Oh, I mean, just in case, I'm sure there won't be a problem."

"Right." Abby grimaced, even though Claire couldn't see her. She sighed. "Okay, okay. I said I would do this, but for the record, I think you're crazy."

"Excuse me, Miss?"

"Hold on a sec," Abby said into the phone, then turned to the frazzled looking woman beside her. "Yes?"

"What's your name, dear?"

"Abby Walker. I'm filling in for Claire Rogers." She held her breath. Would it work or would they turn her away? The thought had some merit. If they wouldn't let her participate, she could go home and forget the whole thing.

The woman marked her clipboard, then nodded. "Sure, no problem." She glanced at the phone in Abby's hand. "Whenever you're set, they're ready for you in makeup."

"Oh, okay. I'll be right there."

"Is your fiancé here yet?"

"My fiancé?" Abby asked. "Um, no, I don't see him yet." Would she recognize him if she did? "He should be here any minute."

"Super." The woman flashed a bright smile, as if glad something were going right. "And his name?"

"Noah."

"What about his last name?"

Last name? Abby went blank. Did she know it? Then through the cell phone she heard, "Grant."

She stifled a giggle and repeated, "Grant," for the woman beside her, who once again checked her clipboard. "Noah Grant."

"Great." The woman made a note with the pencil she'd retrieved from behind one ear. "I'll send him your way as soon as he gets here. Now I really need you to run along. We're on a tight schedule, you know."

"Got it," Abby replied, then spoke into her phone as the woman walked away. "Thanks. By the way, you owe me big time for this one."

"No, thank *you*. I do owe you big time, especially if you win."

"Claire—" Abby began.

"I know it's a long shot, but it could happen. You never know."

"Don't get your hopes up, okay? I said I'd do this, but I'm not making any promises about the outcome."

"I know, I know. I'm just so bummed I can't be there. Of all the rotten luck."

"How is your ankle, by the way?"

"Better. I can put some weight on it today."

"Well, good. Look, I have to go. They need me in makeup." She rolled her eyes.

"Okay, call me as soon as you're done. I want to hear all about it."

"Sure." Abby returned the phone to her purse, then asked a nearby technician where she could find the Green Room. Soon, they had her ensconced in a comfortable swiveling chair. Several people in smocks swarmed around her to apply stage makeup and secure her long brown hair into a simple ponytail.

"Hi, honey. Sorry I'm late."

Abby looked up at the voice, then jumped when warm lips brushed a kiss across her forehead. She stared at the man bent over her. She'd forgotten how drop-dead gorgeous Noah Grant was. Then again, Claire knew how to pick them. His dark blond hair was fashionably messy, styled into careless spikes. Long, curling lashes, the envy of any female, framed deep blue eyes. Broad shoulders filled out his flannel shirt, and well-worn jeans hugged narrow hips and outlined his—

She yanked her gaze from the fly of his pants. Her face warmed. Noah grinned down at her.

"How was the drive here?" He winked and dropped into the chair next to hers.

"I...it was fine," she stammered, thankful when another smocked worker approached and draped Noah with a towel, then applied stage makeup for him as well.

"All set you two. You can wait here until wardrobe is ready for you."

Once they were alone, Noah turned to her. "Nice to see you again." He kept his voice low.

Abby managed a weak smile. "Yeah, you too."

"Hey, I'm sorry you got stuck doing this at the last minute."

"No problem," she lied. "Do you have any idea what this is all about? Claire didn't give me too many details."

Noah shrugged. The action called attention to the wide span of his shoulders. "We have to play some games against other contestants. The winners get an all expense paid wedding trip to Las Vegas or something."

"Wow, I didn't realize you and Claire were that serious."

"We're not." His voice sounded emphatic. "The game show people were at the mall one day, and Claire signed us up."

Typical Claire. Always ready for anything, no matter what came up.

"What happens if you win?"

"You mean what if *we* win?"

"Yeah, I guess." Abby wiped her sweaty palms down her jeans. She liked everything planned and organized. She liked to think things through. The current situation was way out of her comfort zone, but Claire was a good friend, and Abby hated to let her down. Claire had been the one to hold her hand, sometimes literally, through the hellish time when Abby's grandmother had died and her parents were off on the other side of the world. Claire hadn't left her side for a moment. Being on a game show was the least Abby could do for her. She owed her friend a lot more.

"Then we get to take a great vacation."

"What about the wedding part?"

Noah grinned. "We won't take advantage of that part. Wouldn't you like to get away from here and relax at a luxury resort where people cater to your every whim?"

Would he be shocked if she said no? After traveling around the world with her parents while growing up, staying in her cozy house held more appeal than any vacation ever could. She felt settled, and she liked it.

More important than that, the assumption she'd be willing to go, or even be interested in going, on a vacation with a virtual stranger rankled. And what about Claire? Had he forgotten about his girlfriend?

The approach of a harried young man wearing a rumpled shirt and a tie that wasn't quite straight saved her from answering. "Noah Grant and Abby Walker?"

"Yes."

"You'll need to sign these." He handed them each a stack of official-looking documents and scurried off.

She looked through the thick sheaf of papers. "What in the world are these?"

"Probably standard paperwork. You know, saying we'll be on the show and that our likeness will be used, blah, blah, blah." Noah grabbed a pen from a nearby table and signed the papers in quick succession.

"Aren't you even going to read them?"

He looked up. "Nah. I'm sure it's only a formality, bunches of legal jargon."

Not about to sign anything without looking it over carefully, Abby perused the documents. After reading only part of the first page, her head throbbed. She rubbed her temples. Why did lawyers have to use such complicated language? She tried to understand as best she could, but it might as well have been a foreign tongue.

"Done with those?" The harried assistant had returned.

"Sure, here." Noah handed his stack of papers over.

"Um, just a minute," she stalled.

"It's standard stuff, Miss. I really need you to sign them." He looked at his watch. "The show goes on in fifteen minutes."

Against her better judgment, Abby bit her lip and penned her name across the bottom of each page.

The man grabbed them as soon as she finished. "Great. Now if everyone could follow me, we need to get you into your jumpsuits."

"Jumpsuits?" But either he didn't hear her or chose to ignore her.

Her steps dragged as she followed Noah. How had she gotten herself into this? She wanted to kill Claire.

Several minutes later the thought of committing murder lingered. She sat alongside Noah on a high stool, wearing a green jumpsuit, on the set of the game show. Four other couples, each dressed in a different color of the same unflattering outfit, sat nearby. Even Noah didn't look good in the attire. Or at least not as good as he did in his form-fitting jeans.

The stage manager explained how the show worked. Each couple had to perform certain tasks and try to finish before anyone else. After the preliminary round, the two couples with the most points advanced to the final round where they'd have one last task to accomplish. The winners then took off for their dream wedding.

Dream wedding. Right, Abby scoffed to herself. Who in their right mind would dream of a Vegas wedding?

"Now remember," the stage manager said. "We're taping in front of a live studio audience, but the show itself won't be broadcast live. We'll let you know the airdate so you can watch yourselves at home."

"Oh, goody," she muttered under her breath. No way. Living the experience once would be quite enough, thank you very much.

Noah grinned down at her.

"Everyone set?" The manager gave a thumbs-up sign to the nearby camera man.

"Okay then, ready in five, four, three..." He gave the two and one signals silently. A red light appeared at the top of the camera.

Abby's heart hammered against her ribs. A wave of dizziness washed over her, leaving a lightheaded feeling in its wake. She swallowed and clenched her fists. Her nails dug into her palms. Noah reached over and grabbed her hand. She jumped.

"Relax," he said. "It'll be fun."

She glared.

Theme music swelled, and the audience clapped and cheered as the host of the show ran out onto the stage. He flashed his one-hundred-megawatt smile at them, before turning to the camera.

"Howdy, folks. Welcome to another edition of *Win a Wild Wedding Weekend*, the show where couples compete to win the wedding of their dreams. We're glad you've tuned in tonight because you're in for a special night, full of excitement and surprises. Now let's meet our five hopeful couples."

She listened to the questions asked of each couple and the responses they gave. She and Noah were fourth in line, and she didn't want to make any mistakes. But when the host stood in front of them, her mouth went dry. As if sensing her discomfort, Noah gave her hand a reassuring squeeze.

"And here's our fourth couple from right here in Chicago. Please welcome Abby Walker and Noah Grant." He waited for the applause to die down, then turned his ultra bright smile on them. He consulted the index cards in his hand. "Abby, it says here that you're an office manager, and Noah, you're a photojournalist."

"That's right," Noah answered.

"It certainly sounds like an exciting job. You must be used to traveling."

"It's great. I've been all over the world."

"Well, we'll have to come up with something pretty spectacular to impress you." He turned to Abby. "So, how did the two of you meet?"

Her smile faltered, but she recovered in a flash. "A mutual friend set us up."

Noah's lips quirked as if he were trying to repress a grin. She congratulated herself on the half-truth. Claire *had* set them up. But only to be on the stupid show.

"Fabulous. Well, good luck to you." The host moved on, but before the camera panned to follow him, Noah leaned over and brushed his lips against hers.

She never heard what the host said to the last couple. She couldn't hear a thing over the thundering of her heart. The slight touch of his mouth on hers had sent her pulse racing.

"Well, folks, we'll be back in a minute to play *Win a Wild Wedding Weekend*. Don't touch that remote."

"And cut," the director said. "All right everybody, we'll take five and then film the next segment."

"What was that for?" she hissed.

Noah shrugged. "Sorry. Everyone else did it. I

didn't want to be the only couple who didn't kiss."

"Oh." She felt foolish for overreacting , but her response had taken her aback. She'd been kissed before, but she had the feeling a girl would never forget being kissed by Noah Grant, and this hadn't even been a real kiss. She couldn't imagine what it would be like, and she shouldn't try at any rate. Guilt flooded through her as she thought of Claire. What was Claire going to say when she watched the show and saw the kiss, brief as it had been?

The stage manager's voice broke into her thoughts. "Okay, kids, we're back in five."

Forty-five minutes later Abby looked down in dismay. The ugly green of her jumpsuit hid beneath a revolting mixture of sand, whipped cream, and sawdust. A glance at Noah and the other couples showed they had faired no better.

Noah caught her look and grinned. "See, I told you this would be fun."

She glowered at him. Crawling through a plastic swimming pool filled with whipped cream searching for marbles hadn't been her idea of fun.

Her gaze slipped to a dab of the creamy white stuff marring Noah's temple. Without thinking, she reached up and wiped it away, then licked the sweetness from her finger.

His gaze tracked the gesture, then returned to her own.

"You, uh, had some on your face," she hastened to explain. What had prompted the impulsive gesture? And why was he staring at her?

His gaze traveled down her body. "You have it all over you," he said at last.

Abby nodded, unable to speak, caught in the heat of his look. His words sounded intimate, falling over her like a caress. She shivered as he drew a finger down her cheek, removed the whipped cream there, and tasted it as she had done. She swallowed hard.

"Let's get you cleaned up a bit, dear."

It took a moment for the words to register. Giving herself a mental shake, she turned. The same woman who had taken her name before the show stood in front of her. She followed the other woman toward the dressing rooms, but glanced over her shoulder at Noah. He still watched her.

****

Noah's gaze lingered on the gentle sway of Abby's hips as the two women walked away. Even covered in the disgusting mess, wisps of hair stuck to her face, she looked fabulous.

She would photograph well. Not beautiful by today's super-skinny model standards, but her sculpted cheekbones and long curling lashes lent her a classical air. And her eyes were so expressive.

His mouth had gone dry when she'd licked the whipped cream from her finger. He hadn't been able to resist doing the same to her. To see her reaction. He'd wanted to reach for his camera to capture the look. The moment.

His imagination took flight as he envisioned her against vibrant backdrops. What would suit her best? The vivid colors of summer, the soft pastels of spring, or the earthy tones of autumn?

It would be a shame not to see her again once the whole game show thing ended. Abby would be a great subject to work with on film. Any background would suit her. He'd traveled all over the world photographing places and people. Not many could compare to her.

Maybe he'd call her sometime, in a professional sense.

Then he thought of Claire. If there was one thing he knew about women, they didn't take kindly to things like that. He and Claire weren't exclusive or anything. They'd only gone out a couple of times, nothing serious. But he knew better. You didn't mess around with women who were friends with each other.

"And I'm usually up for anything," he muttered to himself.

Twenty minutes later he wanted to eat his words.

"What did you say?" he asked the wardrobe mistress, sure he had misunderstood.

"You get in the suit with your fiancée," the woman repeated.

Seconds ago Abby had emerged from the dressing room wearing another ugly green jumpsuit, this one about ten sizes too big for her. It sagged over her slender frame, drooping almost to the floor.

They were supposed to wear the thing together?

"What?" Abby's face went pale. Her soft green eyes looked enormous in her shocked face.

"Your fiancé gets in too," the woman repeated for the third time. "Let's not waste time. We have a show to get on."

"Oh, no," Abby said. "This is where I draw the line."

The woman looked puzzled. "But you're finalists. You're going to the final round. This is what you need to wear."

Noah glanced down at Abby who looked as if she were going to pass out, then tried to reassure her. "How bad can it be?"

Her eyes went wider still. "You're not seriously considering—"

"Come on, we made it to the final round. We can't back out now. We're already a mess. Let's finish this. See what happens."

"I don't know." She eyed the jumpsuit hanging from her shoulders, then let her gaze rove over his body. "I don't think it will work."

"Come on, there's plenty of room. See?"

He climbed into the jumpsuit with her.

And made an important discovery.

He'd lied. There wasn't plenty of room.

With both of them in it, their bodies pressed intimately close. He felt each breath she took. When the wardrobe mistress zipped up the back, Abby's breasts flattened themselves against his chest.

Their bodies melded together from chest to thigh. Every one of her soft curves imprinted itself on his senses. The beat of her heart accelerated next to his.

Her head came to right beneath his chin. She tipped her head back to meet his gaze, her eyes huge. The expression in them told him she could feel him too.

Her breath hitched, pressing her closer still.

If he didn't get his mind out of the gutter, she'd feel his body's instinctive reaction to her nearness. He wouldn't be able to hide it with her plastered against him.

The wardrobe mistress gave them instructions. Noah tried to concentrate. And think about his grandma in the shower. Anything to keep from dwelling on the soft curves pressed against him.

"Okay, now I know it's a little awkward at first. Pretend you're dancing. That's it. Step together. Sideways now. Great. You've got it."

With slow, shuffling progress they made their way toward the stage. The other finalist couple slipped along beside them.

Once there, the stage manager explained the final rules, and then the cameras rolled. And Noah could almost ignore how perfectly Abby's body fit with his in the confines of the tight suit.

****

"All right, folks, here we go with the final round."

The host's voice came to Abby as if from a long

way away. The sexy scent of Noah's aftershave washed over her. She sucked in a breath in a vain attempt to put some distance between her body and his, but the movement only pressed her breasts tighter against the muscled wall of his chest.

Bad idea.

"You okay?"

She didn't trust her voice, so she shook her head.

The host continued, "For our final task, our couples will have one minute to transfer as many beach balls as they can from this net to the box on the other side of the stage." He paused and turned to them. "Any questions?"

"Can we get this over with?" she muttered. She tried not to move against Noah in the suit.

Could he feel the rapid beat of her heart? No doubt. She felt every breath he took.

"We're almost done. Hang in there," he said. His voice sounded strained.

"All right, couples, take your marks."

She glanced over at the red-suited couple. "Let them win," she whispered to Noah.

He nodded.

"And, go!"

With an awkward shuffle, she and Noah made their way to the net full of beach balls. His thigh flexed against hers with each step. When he stretched to get a ball, his chest brushed hers.

Her pulse accelerated.

They sashayed to the box on one side of the stage. Abby made sure they moved at a slower pace than the red-suits. They repeated the process two more times.

"Ten seconds!"

On the fourth run, the red-suited couple pulled ahead. If they'd had more room in the co-ed jumpsuit, Abby would have sighed in relief.

But then her relief turned to dismay. The other couple slipped and fell, and before she could warn Noah, he put another beach ball into the box.

The buzzer sounded.

She stared at their box, which contained four beach balls, while the red-suited couple's contained three.

Her mouth dropped open. She glanced up at Noah.

He shrugged. His chest rubbed against hers again.

She shrank away from him.

"Well, that does it, folks. Abby Walker and Noah Grant are our big winners today!" The host approached, microphone in hand, megawatt smile in place. "Well, congratulations, you two! You sure made an incredible team out there." He turned and spoke into the camera. "We'll be right back to find out where Abby and Noah will head on their Wild Wedding Weekend!"

"Cut."

The wardrobe mistress hurried over. "Let's get you two out of this suit." She unzipped the back.

Noah climbed out. Abby shoved the offending garment off, then took a step away from him. She hugged herself and rubbed her arms.

"What are we going to do?" she hissed.

He ran his fingers through his hair. "I don't know. We'll figure something out."

"How can you—"

"Okay, folks," the stage manager interrupted. "Let's finish this up. We have one final segment to shoot. We only need Abby and Noah for this one. Here we go."

"Welcome back!" The host bounded onto the stage. "Now the moment you've all been waiting for. Let's find out where our lovebirds are headed."

Abby winced. Her throat went dry.

14

The crowd roared in excitement as the backdrop lit up with a larger than life photograph of a tropical destination.

The scene looked so realistic it seemed as if she'd be able to reach out and touch the palm trees. She could almost taste the salty spray of the ocean on her lips and feel the rough, grainy sand beneath her feet.

"Noah and Abby will be off to Key West, Florida, for a beautiful sunset wedding on the beach. After that they'll sail into paradise for their honeymoon aboard this luxurious cruise ship." The background shifted to a picture of the liner.

The crowd cheered again. Abby pasted a fake smile on her face. Her knees wobbled.

"And now for the surprise you've all been waiting for," the host continued. He grinned at her and Noah.

A lump formed in her throat. What surprise?

"In honor of the one hundredth episode of *Win a Wild Wedding Weekend*, we'll be filming our winning couple's wedding for everyone to see."

The lump fell, settling in the pit of her stomach.

"That's right folks. Be part of the magic as Abby and Noah exchange vows on national TV for the whole world to see. Be sure to stay tuned!"

Chapter Two

"What do you mean we can't get out of it?" A note of hysteria crept into Abby's voice.

"You signed a contract stating you would abide by the rules of the show. You agreed to follow through if you won," the bespectacled man behind the desk explained.

Abby fought down the nausea creeping into her throat and thought back to the large sheaf of papers she had signed. She should have known better.

Noah looked as shell-shocked as she felt. After the host's heart-stopping announcement, the show had ended. As soon as the director yelled *cut*, Noah grabbed her hand and headed toward the producer's office.

"Is there any way to change this?"

"Look, kids. You agreed to be on the show. You signed the contracts."

She gritted her teeth at his condescending tone. "I didn't sign up to be on this show," she grumbled, half to herself.

"What?"

"What my, uh, fiancée means is I wanted to surprise her. She didn't know I was going to sign us up until the last minute," Noah interjected. "She's always dreamed of a big, traditional wedding. Isn't there any way we could turn the prize over to the other couple?"

"I'm sorry. The film's in the can and ready to be edited for broadcast. So, unless you'd like to pay for another show to be shot—"

A spark of hope flared inside Abby. "How much

would that be?"

Her face blanched when the producer named the sum. A glance at Noah revealed the number had stunned him as well.

"Look, kids, I wish there were something I could do, but my hands are tied. You signed the contracts," he repeated for what seemed like the thousandth time.

Noah rose. Abby got to her feet beside him.

"Thanks for your time."

"No problem. We'll be in touch with all of the details for the wedding and the follow-up show."

She gulped. This couldn't be happening. She was not going to marry a man she hardly knew. On national television.

Outside the producer's office, Noah sank against the wall. He tilted his head back and shoved his hands deep into his pockets. She avoided looking at the way the pose thrust his hips forward and watched his face. After a moment, he met her gaze.

"What are we going to do?"

Noah shook his head. "I don't know. I don't have that kind of money."

"Neither do I."

They fell silent. The quiet grated on her nerves until they stretched to the breaking point. "We have to think of something."

"I know. Come on."

"Where are we going?"

"There's a coffee shop across the street. We can get something to drink and talk this over."

Once there, Noah ordered, then tossed several bills down on the counter.

"You don't have to do that. I can pay for my own coffee."

"Hey, can't a guy buy his fiancée a drink?"

Noah's tone teased, but the taut grip Abby had on her emotions snapped. "Stop calling me that. This isn't funny. We cannot get married."

Noah glanced around him. "Shh. Come on, let's sit." He guided her to a small table at the rear of the shop, his hand warm at the small of her back. She slid away from his light touch and into the booth.

Noah tossed his jacket on the seat and scooted in across from her. He regarded her with wary eyes. "I'm sorry," he said. "I was only teasing."

"I know." Abby sighed. "And I'm sorry I snapped at you. But this is all so unbelievable."

Noah sipped his coffee and looked at her, a thoughtful expression on his face. "Maybe it won't be so bad."

She choked on her own coffee. "What?"

"It's not like we're really going to get married."

"That's exactly what they want us to do. 'In honor of the hundredth show,'" she mimicked. "I can't believe people have watched that asinine show a hundred times."

Noah chuckled, the sound warming her more than the hot drink she sipped. "Come on, maybe it'll be fun."

"Fun? That's what Claire said when she talked me into this in the first place." Abby clapped her hand over her mouth. "Oh my gosh. Claire."

"What about her?"

"How are we going to explain to your girlfriend we have to get married?"

"Whoa," Noah said. "Claire's not my girlfriend. We've only been out a couple of times."

"Why in the world did you sign up to be on that ridiculous show if she's not even your girlfriend?"

"I told you. We were at the mall one day, and she thought it looked like fun." His voice held a decided edge.

Abby glared. She'd slug him if he said the word *fun* again. The day was turning out to be anything but.

"And besides, how was I supposed to know we'd win?" Noah sounded defensive.

She bit back a retort. They were getting nowhere. "What are we going to do?"

"I don't think there's anything we can do."

"You're actually suggesting we go through with this?" She set her cup down and massaged her temples.

"I don't see that we have any other choice. Unless you can come up with the exorbitant amount of money to pay for a new show."

"Of course not. But I hardly know you. How can I marry someone I don't know?" Unbidden the memory of being together in the jumpsuit came to mind. She knew what his body felt like pressed close to hers. Her face warmed.

Noah reached across the table and caught her hand in his. She jumped. Had he read her mind?

"We'll have to get to know each other. Besides, like I said, it's not as though we'll really be married. Not like until death do us part. I mean, we'll go on a great vacation, get a cool tan, then come home and get an annulment."

In spite of herself, she smiled, even though her stomach churned. "You have it all worked out, hey?" It did sound simple when he put it in that way. But still, marrying someone she hardly knew?

"Well, I figure, we might as well make the best of the situation. Believe me," he continued, the light teasing tone replaced by earnestness. "If there were any way I could come up with the money, I would do it."

"I know," Abby said. "I—" The chime of her cell phone cut her off. She retrieved it from her purse. "Hello?"

"Hey. So? Did you have fun?" Claire's voice came over the line.

Abby pulled her hand from Noah's as if they

could be seen through the phone. She'd forgotten he held it. "Uh, sure, it was fun." She rolled her eyes.

"So, tell me all about it. I want to know everything. Isn't Noah great?"

"Yeah, sure. Great." She lowered her eyes from the man in question.

"Well? Give me the details. What was it like?"

"Crazy."

"How far did you get?"

"Listen, why don't I come over later and tell you all about it?"

"Great. I'll be here. Come over whenever. And thanks again for agreeing to do this. You're the best."

Abby replaced the phone in her purse. Was Claire still going to think she was the best when she told her she was marrying Noah?

"Claire?"

Abby nodded. She gripped her coffee mug as though it could keep the world from spinning out of control around her. Even the enticing aroma of hazelnut didn't soothe her. "How am I going to tell her?"

"We'll think of something. Maybe she'll get a kick out of it."

Her mouth dropped open. "You can't be serious."

Noah leaned back in the booth, draping his arm across the seat. "Sure, why not? She was the one who asked you to fill in for her in the first place."

"Yes, but I'm sure she never dreamed it would come to this. I never dreamed it would come to this." How could he be so blasé about the whole thing? He looked so relaxed, while her stomach threatened to turn itself inside out.

"So, tell me about yourself."

"What?"

"You said we didn't know each other very well. Let's get to know each other." He studied her.

Her mind spun at the abrupt change in conversation. She shook her head to clear it. "What do you want to know?"

"Anything? Where did you grow up?"

"Everywhere. My dad is in the Navy. We were always moving from place to place."

"That must have been exciting."

"I hated it." She grimaced at the surprised look on his face. "All I ever wanted was to be like other kids. Have a real house with a backyard for the family dog to run around in and friends I didn't have to say good-bye to after a year or two.

"So, after I graduated from high school, I came here to live with my grandma while I went to college. When she died I inherited her house, and I haven't moved since. And that's the way I like it." She took a sip of coffee, which had become tepid. "What about you?"

Noah chuckled. "Well, I'm the opposite of you. I grew up in a small town in Indiana and couldn't wait to get out of there. First chance I could I got in my car and drove out of there and didn't look back."

"Earlier you mentioned you travel all around the world?"

Noah nodded. "I'm a freelance photographer. Sometimes I take pictures and try to sell them. Other times I'm commissioned for specific work. I have an apartment here in the city, so I'm based out of Chicago, but I don't spend a lot of time here. I can't stand staying put."

She shrugged away the odd feeling of disappointment his words brought. "Well, it's a good thing we're not getting married for real. It sounds as if it would never work."

Noah laughed, then shifted in the booth.

The movement drew her attention to the wide expanse of his chest. She knew what it felt like to be crushed against it. Why couldn't she forget how his body felt next to hers?

"What?"

Noah had said something, but she hadn't been listening. She forced herself to look away, dismayed to have been staring.

"My coffee's cold." She slid from the booth. "How about a refill?"

Without waiting for a reply, she grabbed his mug and headed to the counter.

****

Noah watched Abby go, then dropped his head back on top of the cushion behind him. He took a deep breath, then exhaled. He hoped his casual pose belied the tension knotting the muscles in his neck and back. He couldn't believe this was happening.

At thirty-four he wasn't ready to even begin thinking about getting married. He wasn't about to copy his parents' mistakes. They'd been parents many times over by the time they were his age. He didn't plan on repeating history. No sir.

They had married so young. Had kids so young. Had missed out on so many things. Because of him.

His chest tightened.

Well, he wasn't going to miss out on anything. He liked his carefree lifestyle and wasn't about to change it for anything. Or anyone.

That's why he kept trying to assure Abby this was only an adventure. Nothing more. He needed to reassure himself too.

They weren't getting married in the real sense. No settling down and having kids. He broke out in a cold sweat thinking about it.

Like he'd told Abby, they'd take a nice vacation, get an annulment, and go their separate ways. Easy enough. No big deal.

"Here you go."

He looked up as Abby returned with the coffee. "Thanks."

22

"No problem." She slid back into her side of the booth. "It's the least I can do for my fiancé."

She teased, as he had done earlier, but the words made his mouth go dry. He gulped his drink, the hot liquid searing his throat.

"We're really going to do this?"

"Yeah, I guess so."

Abby stared at him for a moment, her eyes apprehensive. She sipped her coffee. "What are you going to tell people?"

"Nothing."

"Nothing? What if they see the show?"

"I'm hoping anyone I know will have better taste than to watch it."

She laughed. The sound washed over him in pleasurable waves.

"What about you? Are you going to tell your family?"

Abby shook her head. The movement scattered her long, brown hair across her shoulders. It caught the sunlight streaming in through the nearby window, highlighting the strands with streaks of reddish gold. Noah's hands itched for his camera.

"No way. Dad's stationed in Okinawa right now, so there's not much chance they'll catch it."

He tore his gaze away from her shimmering hair. "Uh, right. Sure."

"Now we wait for the studio to contact us with details?"

"Yeah, that sounds about right."

"And I have to tell Claire." Abby's eyes reflected her worry.

He reached across the table and took her hand in his. He stroked the back of it absentmindedly. "We'll tell her together."

"That's not necessary. You don't have to—"

"I want to," he cut in. "I'm a part of this too. Remember?"

Abby glanced down at their joined hands. "How can I forget?"

The question didn't need an answer, and Noah would have been hard pressed to come up with one anyway.

How had they gotten into this mess?

****

In the elevator heading toward Claire's apartment, Abby took a deep breath. How in the world were they going to break the news?

She glanced over at Noah, who like her had fallen silent when the doors closed. He looked calm and unaffected, as if he didn't have a care in the world. She wished she could say the same. Butterflies danced in her stomach. She kept hoping she'd wake up from the bizarre dream she was having.

But Noah's presence beside her was all too real. They stood close in the small elevator. The smell of his aftershave surrounded her, tickling her nose with its crisp scent. When he shifted his feet, his arm brushed hers. She tried not to look at him.

So she glued her eyes to the ascending numbers above the door.

She couldn't be considering marrying this man. This stranger.

Someday she wanted to meet someone and settle down. Then she'd have everything she'd always wished for. Right down to the white picket fence and the family dog.

But not like this. Never like this, and especially not with someone like Noah. She wanted someone who would settle down with her. Not be off to all corners of the world on a whim. One lifetime of that had been quite enough.

But then again, they weren't settling down. Like Noah had said, it wasn't like this was 'til death us do part. They'd be married for a week. Then they'd each go on with their own lives—she back to her cozy house in the suburbs, and Noah back to his adventures.

Noah jarred her from her thoughts with a nudge from his shoulder. "Hey."

"Hey."

He grinned. "Don't worry, it's going to be okay."

She made a face at him. "You keep saying that."

"Because it's the truth."

She must have still looked skeptical because he added, "Really."

"I guess the only thing we can do is get this over with and then move on with our lives." Abby voiced the thoughts that spun around in her head.

Noah nodded in agreement as a soft ding signaled they'd reached their destination. The doors slid open.

She hesitated. She couldn't do this. How would Claire react?

"Come on." Noah grabbed her hand and tugged her out of the elevator. She ignored the unwelcome spark his touch generated.

All too soon they reached Claire's apartment.

Abby bit her lip.

Noah squeezed the hand he held. "You okay?"

She nodded even though her heart raced.

Before they could knock, the door opened and Claire poked her head out. "Took you long enough," she began, then stopped when she saw Noah. "What are you doing here?" Her gaze dropped to their joined hands. She frowned.

Abby let go of Noah's hand. She shook off the sudden feeling of loss and faced her friend. "We have to talk to you about something."

Chapter Three

Claire looked from Abby to Noah, then stepped back, opening the door wider. "Sure, come on in."

Once inside Claire greeted Abby with a hug and Noah with a kiss. Abby looked away at the intimate gesture, but not before she'd seen the wary look in Noah's eyes. The first glimpse she'd gotten that he was as uncomfortable with the situation as she was.

The trio stood, not speaking.

Claire broke the silence. "Well, come on. Tell me all about it. I'm so bummed I missed it." Her eyes flicked back and forth between Abby and Noah.

They made their way into the living room. Claire hobbled to a chair by the window. She propped her elastic wrapped foot on the ottoman. Noah took the sofa. Abby had no choice but to join him there, so she sat as far from him as possible.

"Come on, guys. What happened? I'm dying here."

Abby glanced at Noah, feeling as if she was going to throw up.

He shrugged. "It was fun."

She glared at the word and the man who had uttered it. "It was not fun. It was ridiculous. They made us find marbles in swimming pools filled with whipped cream."

Claire laughed. "It sounds messy, that's for sure."

"And we had to wear these awful jumpsuits." Abby didn't mention they'd had to wear one together. Her face heated from the memory.

"So, what was the prize? The information I got

at the mall said the winning couple got a trip to Vegas or something." Claire's voice sounded odd, almost wistful.

"Actually this time it's a trip to Key West and a cruise," Noah answered.

"Wow," Claire breathed. "Too bad you didn't win. What a great trip."

Abby remained silent, not daring to look at Noah.

"Well, actually," he began.

"You're kidding? You guys really won? We get to go to Key West?" Claire nearly bounced out of her chair. She looked expectantly at Noah.

He frowned at her words. "Not exactly."

Abby winced.

Claire looked puzzled. "But you just said—"

"There's a little more to it."

"What do you mean?"

Noah looked at Abby, but she shook her head, still feeling sick. She couldn't tell Claire. Thank goodness Noah had insisted on coming along.

"Well, Abby and I won, so—"

"Oh, yeah, so we'll have to change the names again. Oh well, we did it once. It shouldn't be a problem."

Something in the tone of Claire's voice sent a shiver of unease through Abby. Claire sounded too excited. "Look, Claire, you don't understand. We can't change names." She took a deep breath and blurted, "Noah and I have to get married."

A moment of shocked silence met her outburst.

Then Claire's laughter broke in, but it sounded forced. "That's ridiculous. What do you mean, you and Noah have to get married?"

"It's like this." Noah explained the whole hundredth episode surprise, the film that had been shot, and the binding contracts they'd signed.

"Oh," Claire said when he finished. She sat back

in her chair, then looked from one to the other.

The hint of anger in her eyes surprised Abby.

"It's all my fault," Noah said. "I signed those contracts without really looking at them, and I convinced Abby to do the same."

"I should have looked them over. It's as much my fault as it is yours." For some inexplicable reason Abby wanted to defend him.

"What are you going to do? I mean, it's not like you're really going to get married." Claire's tone made the words sound more like a question.

Abby glanced at Noah once again. "We've been over this a hundred times. There's not much we can do."

"So," Noah picked up the thread of conversation. "We're going to get married, and then as soon as we get back home, we'll get an annulment."

"You're going through with it? With the marriage?" The excitement in Claire's voice had faded, replaced by a note of disbelief.

Noah nodded. "Looks that way."

Claire shook her head. "But that's impossible. The two of you can't get married." She sounded on the edge of losing control.

"We tried to get out of it," Abby hastened to clarify. "We wanted to give the prize to the other couple, but we weren't able to."

"Forget the other couple. It's my prize. Give it to me. It was my idea to go on that show. I—"

"We can't," Noah interrupted. "They filmed us," he nodded toward Abby, "as the winners. Everything's on tape."

"Can't they just film again?"

"We asked," Abby assured Claire, even though the question hadn't been addressed to her. In fact Claire had avoided looking at her. "They wouldn't do it. Too much money involved."

"Can't you pay for it yourselves?"

"I don't have that kind of money." Noah sounded impatient now. "Look, Abby and I have been through this. We don't have a choice."

Claire didn't look convinced. "There has to be another way."

Silence descended once again until Noah cleared his throat. He looked at his watch and stood. "I really need to get going."

Abby didn't blame him for wanting to escape. The tension in the room was palpable.

Claire rose from her chair as well. "I'll walk you out." She cast an enigmatic look at Abby.

Noah hesitated. "Uh, sure," he said.

At the door Claire pulled his face down to hers and kissed him. Not a chaste peck on the lips, but a deep, intimate, open-mouthed kiss. She pressed up against him and wrapped her arms around his neck.

Claire was staking her claim.

Fine with Abby. Claire could have Noah. Abby wasn't interested in him. He wasn't her type at all.

Noah disentangled himself from Claire's embrace. His gaze flicked to Abby.

She averted her eyes.

"Jesus, Claire," Noah muttered. He sounded uncomfortable.

"Call me later," Claire said. She smoothed her hand down his jaw.

Without replying, Noah turned and walked out the door.

Claire pivoted, keeping her weight off her injured foot, to face Abby, a smug look on her face. Then her gaze hardened.

"So, how did all of this really happen? Were you *trying* to win?"

The accusatory note in Claire's voice took Abby by surprise. "No, of course not."

"I still don't understand how you and Noah could win a game for couples."

Abby bit back a sigh. "It wasn't like that. I mean they didn't ask us a bunch of questions about each other. We played weird games. Like we told you, we crawled through kiddie pools and stuff like that. It was just dumb luck that we made it to the final round."

Claire snorted.

Abby blinked. "Really. And then we decided to let the other couple win."

"Well that didn't work out so well, did it?"

"It was a mistake."

"Right." Claire folded her arms across her chest. "Did you do it for spite or out of jealousy? Is it that I always have a boyfriend and you never do?"

The shock of the words hit Abby like a slap in the face. She stood. "I can't believe you said that. I went on that show as a favor. To you." She blinked back tears. "I wanted to do something for you. You've always been there for me, and I wanted to help you for a change. So when you asked me to fill in for you, I figured it was the least I could do. It didn't even come close to paying you back for all the times you've been there for me, but I wanted to do it. For you."

"Yeah, well don't do me any more favors."

"If I could turn the prize over to you I would. I don't *want* to marry Noah."

"Right." Claire limped from the room.

Abby stared after her friend, heartsick at the conversation they'd just had. She'd known Claire would be upset, but she hadn't realized how upset.

Claire was her best friend in the whole world.

Or at least she had been.

Abby had the feeling that things were never going to be the same again.

****

Arriving home from work several days later, Abby found a large manila envelope in her mailbox with the TV studio's return address on it. A cold knot formed in her stomach.

While the thought of the wedding was never far from her mind, having this physical proof in her hand was like a splash of cold water in the face. She didn't want to look at the contents of the package.

Taking it inside, she tossed it on the kitchen table, putting off opening it for the moment. She changed from her work clothes into comfortable jeans and a T-shirt. On her way back into the kitchen, the phone rang.

She grabbed the receiver and tucked it beneath her ear, opening the fridge and grabbing a bottle of water at the same time. "Hello?"

"Abby? It's Noah."

The identification was unnecessary. Although they hadn't spoken since he'd left Claire's apartment days earlier, she'd recognized the deep timbre of his voice right away.

"Hi." Not the most original response in the world, but what was she supposed to say to the stranger she was going to marry?

"How are you?" The note of concern in his voice touched her.

"Okay, I guess. I'm trying to figure out how all of this is going to work."

"Yeah, me too." Noah paused. "Listen, I've been going over numbers in my head, and I can't—"

"I know," she interrupted. "Neither can I. We've been through this already."

"Did you get the information the studio sent?"

Her gaze slid to the envelope lying on her table. "Something came in the mail today. I haven't opened it yet."

"I got mine today too. They, uh, want us to leave three weeks from Saturday."

"What?" The bottle almost slipped from her hand. "So soon?"

31

"Apparently they're on a really tight schedule so they can run the shows during final sweeps this season. We're going to be the season finale."

"Oh. Great." She had known it would happen soon, but hadn't thought it would be *this* soon. The sick feeling in the pit of her stomach she'd struggled to ignore over the last several days came back with a vengeance.

"Will you be able to get time off work on such short notice?"

She sank down into one of the kitchen chairs. "It shouldn't be a problem. My boss, Jenn, is great. How about you?"

"I have to reschedule a shoot, but other than that I'm free as a bird. One of the perks of being my own boss."

"Oh, right."

"I know you haven't read your information yet, but we have some things to take care of before we go."

"Okay."

"We have to bring our passports and drivers' licenses to the studio so they can copy them and get the ball rolling in Florida for our marriage license."

"Marriage license?"

"We have to have one to make everything legal."

"Of course," she said, a touch of sarcasm in her voice. "Wouldn't want to do anything out of the ordinary."

Noah laughed. "Anyway, they'd like it to be done at least ten days before the wedding, so that doesn't give us much time. I thought maybe we could have lunch tomorrow and take care of it then."

"That sounds okay, but lunch isn't necessary."

"I know it's not necessary, but I'd like to spend some more time with you before..."

Noah left the sentence unfinished, but the thought completed itself in Abby's head. Before they got married.

Her stomach rolled. She swallowed. "Sure. Lunch sounds fine."

"Great. Do you want me to pick you up at work or meet somewhere?"

"Why don't we meet somewhere near the studio."

"That sounds good. I'll call you at work in the morning."

"Okay." She gave him the number.

"See you tomorrow, then."

"Sure, see you tomorrow."

She hung up the phone and stared out the window. How had life gotten so complicated?

****

Noah spotted Abby outside the small café right away. What was it about her that made her stand out from the crowd? She was looking the other way and hadn't seen him approach, so he touched her arm.

She jumped and turned to face him.

"Sorry," he said. "I didn't mean to startle you."

She laughed, but it didn't sound natural. "No, it wasn't you. I was lost in thought."

"Three guesses as to what you were thinking about."

This time her laugh was genuine. "And you'd only need one of those guesses, right?"

"Probably." He inclined his head toward the restaurant. "Do you want to eat first or go to the studio?"

"Let's eat. I'm starved."

"Great." He put his hand on the small of her back, guiding her into the building. The soft, lilac scent of her shampoo drifted to his nostrils when she turned her head to say something over her shoulder.

Once they were seated he took a closer look at her. Her vibrant eyes looked tired. Dark smudges shadowed the lower lids.

"You haven't been sleeping well." The thought bothered him, although he couldn't quite put his finger on why. After all, he'd lain awake the past several nights as well.

She lowered her eyes, but didn't deny his claim.

He reached across the table for her hand. Once again he couldn't stop himself from touching her. He wanted to tell her how sorry he was they had gotten mixed up in the mess they were in, but he'd said the words so many times, they held no real weight anymore. He sighed.

"We need to stop beating ourselves up about this." Abby's soft voice broke the silence that had fallen. She met his gaze. "I mean, we're not getting anywhere, and it's making us crazy."

"That's for sure." Wasn't he supposed to be the one doing the reassuring? But he liked that she was concerned about him.

Abby sighed and fidgeted with her fork.

"Is something else bothering you? You seem distracted."

She met his gaze for a brief second before lowering her lashes. "It's nothing."

"Come on, you can tell me. Maybe I can help."

She shook her head. "I don't think so. It's just, well"—her gaze darted to his again before flicking away—"Claire's still really mad at me."

"Oh."

"Yeah, she won't answer any of my calls. She, um, she thinks I did this on purpose."

"Did what on purpose?"

"Won that game show. So I'd get to marry you."

"What?" Shock tinged the word.

"Yeah. She's not too happy with me at the moment." She paused. "Have you talked to her?" The question came out hesitant, as if she were afraid to ask it.

Noah leaned his head back against the booth. "Yeah, I talked to her this morning. She called to see if I wanted to have lunch." His head came up again so he could make eye contact with Abby. "I told her I couldn't because I was having lunch with you."

"Oh."

The single word sounded so sad he wanted to kick himself. "I'm sorry. I guess I made it worse."

Abby shook her head. "I don't think it can get any worse."

"What if I talked to her? I'll explain everything again."

"I don't think it will make any difference. I told her that I'd turn the prize over to her if I could, but that didn't seem to help either. And of course, that's impossible anyway."

For a moment Noah felt a selfish stab of relief. As bizarre as it was to be marrying Abby, the thought of marrying Claire was unimaginable.

Although he couldn't put his finger on why, being involved with Abby in all of this made it easier to bear.

Then he looked at the sad expression in her eyes, and his heart twisted. He hated to see her suffer.

He squeezed her hand. "I'm sorry," he repeated. "I don't know what to say. I wish there were something I could do to fix things between you and Claire."

"I'm sure things will work themselves out eventually."

By the tone of Abby's voice, Noah could tell she wasn't so sure.

"Have you decided yet?"

Noah looked up at the waitress. "Uh, no, sorry. We haven't even looked yet."

She harrumphed and turned on her heel.

Abby giggled. "Well, now she's a breath of fresh

air, isn't she?"

Noah smiled, heartened that she'd found something to laugh about, then squeezed her hand one more time before releasing it. He grabbed a menu and passed it to her. He opened his own. "What looks good to you?"

****

After they'd finished and the waitress had dropped the check off on their table, Noah pulled out his wallet. As he opened it, Abby's gaze fell on one of the photographs inside. A plump, blond little girl grinned out of the picture.

"Who's that?"

Noah smiled. "My niece, Taylor."

"Oh, she's adorable." She studied the picture Noah passed to her. "How old is she?"

"Four."

"Do you have any other nieces or nephews?"

Noah nodded. "I have nine."

"Wow. You're so lucky."

"Yeah, well the Grants have a tradition of having babies early on."

"What?" She didn't understand his cryptic comment or the hard tone of his voice.

"Never mind. No nieces and nephews for you, I take it?"

She sighed. "No, I'm an only child." She looked at the picture one last time before handing it back to Noah. "What about you?"

"I have two brothers and two sisters."

"It must have been great growing up with such a big family."

He shrugged. "It was okay."

"Okay?" His blasé tone shocked her. She would have given anything to have one brother or sister around when she was growing up. "Well, it sounds like heaven to me."

"I think traveling around the world like you did

36

would have been great growing up. All we ever did was go to the Wisconsin Dells every other summer. I was so jealous when other kids talked about going to Disney World or the Grand Canyon."

Abby laughed, although her heart contracted at the bitterness in his voice. "What's the old saying? The grass is always greener?"

"Yeah, I guess so."

"At any rate, someday I want to have a home full of kids. And a house with a white picket fence around it."

"The American dream, huh? With the family cat sitting on the front porch?" Noah shuddered.

"Definitely not. The family dog will be running around in the back yard," she corrected. She took a sip of her water. "Do you want to have kids? Add to the Grant tradition?"

"No," he said, almost before she'd completed the question. "I have too much I want to do for me. I don't want to be tied down to a wife and kids. I want to be able to do what I want, go where I want, whenever I want to."

"Oh." Abby didn't know what to say to Noah's emphatic declaration. For her she had always assumed she'd find someone, settle down, and have lots of babies. She couldn't imagine not wanting to have any kids at all.

She studied the man sitting across from her.

He was like all the others she'd dated. Out for some fun, no commitments, no ties, looking for a good time. Although she should have been used to it, disappointment coursed through her, hearing the words from him.

He looked at his watch. "We'd better hustle if we're going to make it to the studio."

Abby had been so caught up in the lunch and conversation, she'd almost forgotten the real purpose of their time together. Noah's words brought it all rushing back.

"Yeah, sure." She reached for her purse. "Do you want to split the check?"

"Nope. My treat."

"Noah."

"Don't 'Noah' me. You can pay next time we go out."

"But—"

"No buts." Noah slid from his side of the booth, tossed some bills on the table, and grabbed her hand. "Come on." He pulled her from her seat.

Ten minutes later they sat facing the producer of the game show.

"Thanks for coming down today, kids. First we need to take care of the basic paperwork. I need to see a driver's license and a birth certificate from each of you."

She and Noah produced the requested identification.

"Great, then I have a few questions, and you can be on your way. Miss Walker, will you be changing your name to Grant?"

"No."

The man nodded, then marked something on the paper in front of him. "You know in my day, it really wasn't an option. Women were expected to take their husband's name."

She bristled at the remark, but Noah cut in. "Abby and I discussed the matter, and we decided it would be better this way.

The producer shrugged as if to say it didn't matter one way or another to him, then excused himself to make copies of their documents.

They sat in awkward silence. She had run out of platitudes, or anything else, to say. Finally the producer returned, handed them their things, and, after indicating he'd be in touch with more details soon, sent them on their way.

Within moments they stood on the sidewalk outside the studio.

Noah broke the painful silence. "Well, thanks for meeting me."

"No problem. Thanks for lunch."

"My pleasure. I guess I'll talk to you soon?"

She nodded. "I have to get back to work."

"Sure. Have a good rest of the day."

She smiled and turned to walk away, but Noah's voice stopped her.

"Abby?"

She looked back at him, but before she could ask what he wanted, he reached out and brushed a lock of hair from her forehead.

The light touch of his skin against hers sent a frisson of awareness through her.

Then he tangled his fingers through the strands and tilted her face up toward him. She'd barely guessed his intent before his mouth descended and captured hers. His lips stroked over hers. His warm breath moistened the sudden dryness of hers.

Her pulse accelerated as he deepened the kiss. Tingling heat spread through her limbs, chasing away the chill of the wintry air around her.

Long seconds later he pulled back to look at her. His eyes probed hers.

He smiled a half smile. "See you later." And then he was gone.

Abby stood. Her body trembled. Her heart pounded. Her mind raced. Why in the world had Noah kissed her?

Chapter Four

Abby took a deep breath and slowly exhaled.

Since Claire refused to take her phone calls, she'd decided a stronger course of action was needed. She'd headed over to Claire's apartment.

Luck had been with her. She'd caught someone on the way out of the main door downstairs and hadn't needed to be buzzed up. She was pretty sure Claire would have refused to let her in.

Now she stood outside the apartment. Would Claire slam the door in her face?

Only one way to find out.

She pulled a final fortifying breath into her lungs and knocked.

"Oh, it's you." Claire sounded less than enthusiastic to see Abby standing in the hallway.

Although Abby had expected the reaction, she still felt a stab of disappointment. "Can we talk?"

Claire folded her arms across her chest. "I really don't think there's anything to talk about."

"May I come in? Please?"

After a moment, Claire stepped back. "Suit yourself. But I don't have a lot of time. I have a date tonight." She sounded smug.

Abby moved past Claire into the apartment. "Oh, that's nice." She glanced down. "How's your ankle?"

"Fine. Look, Noah's coming to pick me up around seven. Can we make this quick?"

Her date was with Noah? No wonder she'd sounded smug.

Abby pushed away a niggle of unease. Claire

having a date with Noah was a good thing. So why did it make Abby feel so funny inside?

"Yeah," Claire continued when Abby didn't respond. "Just because you guys won that game show doesn't mean Noah and I can't go out anymore. I mean, he was mine first."

Abby bit back a sigh. "He's still yours, Claire. I don't want him."

"No, you're just going to marry him, that's all."

"Not because I want to. Because I have to. Because of that stupid show."

"That stupid show worked out pretty nicely for you, Abby. I mean, normally, you wouldn't get a guy like Noah."

Abby ignored the stab the words caused. Claire was hurt and lashing out.

"Admit it, you're enjoying every minute of this."

"Hardly."

"Yeah, right. What did you do for lunch the other day?"

Of course she'd bring that up. "We had to take care of some things at the studio. Lunch wasn't any big deal." She pushed away the memory of Noah's kiss and hoped Claire wouldn't see her telltale blush. If Claire ever found out Noah had kissed her, she'd never speak to her again.

"Well don't think this marriage of yours is going to last. I know what kind of man Noah is, and he's not the type of guy to want to settle down and get married."

"I know that."

"Then maybe you should let him off the hook?"

Abby couldn't believe her ears. "Let him off the hook? Look, Claire, we've told you, we tried to get out of this, to get 'off the hook' as you put it. They won't let us. We're stuck. I'm sorry this all happened, but we didn't do it on purpose."

"Just listen to yourself, Abby. *We* tried to do

this, and they won't let *us*. You talk as if you and Noah are a couple. Which is probably what you're angling for anyway."

Abby gritted her teeth. "For the last time, I don't want to be with Noah."

"Sure. Of course you don't. Why would any woman want to be with him? After all he's only gorgeous and smart. Not to mention his fabulous car and great job. But you already know that. That's why you keep trying to *fix* the situation."

"Look, we're—I'm"—she hastily corrected at the look on Claire's face—"in this situation because you asked me to be. I never would have been on that show with Noah in the first place if you hadn't asked me to fill in."

Claire crossed her arms over her chest. "Oh, so now this is all my fault?"

Abby fought the urge to scream. "No, I'm not saying that. What I'm saying is that this is one big giant mix up, and I hate to see our friendship get ruined because of it."

"It's a little too late for that, don't you think? Maybe you should have thought more about our friendship before you decided to marry Noah."

"That's just it. I never *decided* to do anything. I got stuck on that game show, and now I'm stuck marrying a man I hardly know." The conversation kept going round and round and never went anywhere. How many ways could she say the same thing?

"Oh, come off it. The reluctant bride routine is getting a little old."

"It's not a routine," Abby said quietly. "I don't want to do this, Claire."

"Then don't."

"There's no way out. We signed binding contracts."

"Yeah, I've heard all of this before. And you tried

to lose the final round. And you tried to turn the prize over to the other couple. Blah, blah, blah."

"Claire, I—"

"Look, Noah should be here any minute. Maybe it's time for you to go. I'm sure it would be uncomfortable for you to see your *fiancé* coming to pick up his girlfriend for a date."

Abby sighed. The bitter note in Claire's voice chipped at her soul.

For a long time Claire had been the one person that Abby confided in, told all her troubles to. Now that was ruined. Maybe forever. She didn't think Claire would ever forgive her.

On the one hand she couldn't blame her. After all, she was marrying Claire's boyfriend, even though Noah frowned at the label. It couldn't be easy knowing your best friend was marrying the guy you'd been dating.

But for Claire to think she'd orchestrated everything on purpose, that Abby wanted to marry Noah? That made it even harder to bear.

Nothing she said made any difference. Coming to see Claire had gotten her nowhere.

Her former best friend still wouldn't listen to reason, but Claire was right about one thing. Abby didn't want to be there when Noah arrived.

She hadn't talked to him since he'd kissed her after their appointment at the studio. The thought of seeing him, especially under these circumstances, caused her insides to do flips.

At the door she turned. "Claire?"

"What?" Impatience edged Claire's voice.

Abby shook her head. "Never mind. Have a good time tonight."

"Oh, we will. You can count on it." She closed the door.

A vision of Claire kissing Noah good-bye the other day flashed into Abby's head. She had no doubt as to the kind of fun Claire would have with Noah that night.

The thought was...unsettling, but she couldn't put her finger on why.

Claire had never been secretive about the fact that she slept with many of the men she dated. Abby had never judged her for it. It had never bothered her before.

But this time was different.

Was it because Noah had kissed her too?

Not in the blatantly sexual way Claire had kissed him. But in a sweet, tender way that Abby couldn't forget. Even the memory made her limbs tingle.

Would he kiss Claire that way later?

A hollow ache consumed her.

She sighed and aimed her weary feet in the direction of the elevator.

Life sure had gotten complicated recently.

****

As she was about to jump in the shower the next night, the phone rang.

"Hello?"

"Abby? Hi. It's Noah."

The sound of his voice caused a quiver in her belly. The soft velvet tones brought to mind his kiss. His puzzling, mind numbing, knee-weakening kiss.

Why couldn't she stop thinking about it?

"Uh, hi."

"How are you?"

She pushed away the memory of his lips against hers. "Fine," she lied.

"What have you been up to?"

"Not much. Work. The usual." What was with the small talk?

"Yeah, me too."

"Did you have fun on your date with Claire last night?" The question slipped out before she could

44

stop it. Might as well get it out in the open that she knew he was still seeing Claire. Not that it mattered. But no need to add to the awkwardness of the situation by having to keep that secret.

"My what?" Even through the phone she sensed his confusion.

"Your date with Claire last night."

"I didn't have a date with Claire last night."

"Oh." Now it was Abby's turn to be perplexed.

"Why did you think I went out with Claire?"

"When I talked to her the other day, she said you were on your way over. That you two were going to dinner." She didn't add what else Claire had implied.

"I haven't seen Claire since that day at her apartment when we told her about winning the show."

"Oh. I guess I must have misunderstood." The words weren't true. Claire had lied. Abby's heart sank.

Abby and Noah might have won the game show, but it was Claire who was playing games now. What was she trying to prove? What had she hoped to gain? Abby had told her time and time again she had no interest in Noah.

"Abby? Are you still there?"

She jerked her attention back to him. "Sorry."

"Are you okay?" His voice held an edge of concern.

She shook herself. "Do you really want me to answer that?" She tried to inject a touch of humor into her tone.

He laughed, then became serious. "But you saw Claire. That's great. Did you patch things up?"

"Not really. Because she wouldn't answer my calls, I went over to her place, but it didn't do any good. She's still really upset." She paused. "Have you talked to her?"

"Not since the day she wanted to go out for lunch and I couldn't go because I was meeting you."

The day he'd kissed her.

Heat suffused her face. She was glad he couldn't see her through the phone.

Once again she forced the memory away.

"She's left a couple of messages, but I haven't had the chance to call her back."

"Oh. Maybe you should give her a call," she hinted. If Noah talked to her, maybe Claire would believe *him* about everything that was going on. Or not going on as it were.

Instead of replying to Abby's comment, he changed the subject. "At any rate, I was just calling to let you know that I'll be out of town for a couple of weeks. Probably up until right before the wed—the trip. It'll be tricky to get a hold of me, but, if you need something, you can try my cell."

"Oh, okay." She wrote down the number he recited.

"I'm sorry to leave you alone to deal with all of the last minute details, but I needed to reschedule a couple of photo shoots to meet a deadline."

"No problem. I mean, there's really not much to do. The studio's taking care of everything."

"Oh, right. Have you heard from them lately?"

"No, but I didn't really expect to. I think they have everything they need from us."

After a few more minutes of chitchat that grated on Abby's nerves, Noah signed off.

She hung up the phone with a sigh. Noah being out of town wouldn't help things with Claire. Claire desperately wanted to go out with him. If he was out of town, that would be impossible.

****

Noah stared into space after hanging up the phone. He frowned.

It bothered him that Claire was treating Abby so

poorly. It wasn't Abby's fault she'd gotten caught up in the mess they were in.

The wistful note in her voice when she spoke of Claire tugged at his heart. He wanted to make everything okay again, but didn't have the power to do that.

He'd been avoiding Claire's phone calls. He knew she wanted to get together. Go out.

But it didn't seem right going on a date with Claire when he and Abby would be getting married in a few short weeks.

He shuddered at the thought.

Married.

He was getting married.

As much as possible he avoided thinking about it. When he did think about it, he reminded himself it wasn't real.

But the real pain in Abby's voice made him want to take the hurt away.

Would calling Claire make things better or worse? Probably worse, since the only thing he'd be telling her was he didn't want to see her anymore. Would he be feeling differently about Claire if Abby hadn't taken her place on the show? He didn't think so.

Claire had been someone fun to hang around with, but he didn't see a long term relationship developing. Of course he wasn't interested in a long term relationship with anyone.

But even before the whole game show thing had blown up in their faces and tossed everything into utter chaos, he'd been feeling that it was time to move on. Claire was nice and all. Great personality. Good head on her shoulders. Pretty. But that was it.

He didn't feel anything for Claire.

But for Abby, things were different. She loved Claire. And she was suffering because of it.

The least he could do was give Claire a call. Set

the record straight once and for all. Maybe then she'd stop blaming Abby.

With a sigh he flipped open his cell phone to search for Claire's number. Funny. He hadn't had to look up Abby's when he'd called her a few minutes ago.

"Claire," he said when she answered. "It's Noah."

"Noah. I'm so glad you called."

He winced at the eagerness in her voice. This might be harder than he thought.

"I've tried calling you," she went on, "but I always get your voicemail."

"Uh, yeah, sorry. I've been really busy."

"Oh, that's okay. Maybe we could get together tonight? For drinks or something. Or you could come over to my place and—"

"Sorry. I can't tonight. I'm heading out of town tomorrow and have a lot of last minute things to get together." Part of that was true.

"Oh." Her disappointment filtered through the phone. "Well maybe we can get together when you get back."

"Do you really think that's a good idea?"

"What do you mean?"

Did he need to spell it out? "I mean," he said deliberately, "with everything going on, don't you think it would be kind of weird?"

"Everything that's going on?"

Was she playing dumb on purpose? "Abby and I are getting married," he reminded her. He ignored the trepidation that settled over him at the words.

"Oh, that." Claire laughed, but the sound was off. "I haven't even been thinking about that. It's all for pretend, so what does it matter? Or has Abby tried to convince you that it's real?"

"Why would she do that?"

"Well, I'm sure she's hoping that it will turn into

something."

He gritted his teeth. "At the risk of repeating myself, why would she do that?"

"Why wouldn't she do that? This is a great opportunity for someone like Abby."

"Someone like Abby?" Anger tinged his voice at Claire's implication.

"Well, you know, she's not like us. Abby takes life very seriously. She'd take marriage seriously too. I'm sure she's hoping that something will come out of this. Something permanent."

"You really think that?"

"Believe me, I've been friends with her for a long time. She's always dreamed about getting married and settling down. Now that she's getting married, I'd bet anything she's thinking about the settling down part too."

Although Noah knew what Claire was trying to do, her words sent a frisson of unease down his spine. Was Abby thinking that? Hoping for that?

No. He couldn't make himself believe that. He hadn't known Abby for as long as Claire had, but over the last couple weeks, he'd gotten to know a little about her. He knew one thing for certain.

Abby was not happy about having to marry him.

"I think you're wrong," he responded.

"I hope I am. For your sake. And Abby's," she added, although it sounded like an afterthought. "I'd hate to see her think you two would ever try to make this work for real. I mean, she's not your type at all. I'm really sorry you got stuck with her."

"Stuck with her?" Noah tightened his grip on the phone. Did Claire know how lucky she was they weren't having this conversation in person? If she were there in the room with him, he might not be able to control the urge to shake her.

"Well, I mean stuck marrying her. You know, since we'd signed up and all. Maybe it would be easier if you and I were getting married."

"How would that be easier?" He didn't want to marry anyone, but the more he talked to Claire the more certain he was he didn't want to go out with her anymore, let alone marry her. For pretend or not.

Her friendship with Abby puzzled him. They seemed as different as two people could be. Abby was kind and compassionate and genuine, while Claire on the other hand seemed self-absorbed and insensitive.

"I just mean that you and I would, of course, be aware that it was all for fun. A lark. Something to laugh about over drinks someday."

Noah had had enough of the conversation, but still hadn't gotten around to the real purpose of his call. "Look, Abby's feeling really awful about all of this."

"Right."

He ignored her. "Why don't you give her a call? Talk things out."

"Is that why you called? Because of her?"

He bit back a sigh. "She misses you."

Silence fell.

"Think about it," he said finally. "I know she'd like to hear from you."

Claire made a noncommittal noise.

"I need to get going. I have a lot to do tonight."

"Sure. Um, do you want to get together when you get back from your trip?"

"I'm leaving for Key West as soon as I get back," he said gently. He honestly didn't want to hurt Claire. Hadn't the whole situation caused enough pain? But he hoped she'd take the hint. If he told her he didn't want to see her anymore, she'd find a way to blame Abby. And he definitely didn't want to cause Abby anymore heartache.

"Oh. I see."

"I'm sorry, Claire."

She cleared her throat. "No...uh, no problem. I guess I'll see you around sometime, then?"

He didn't respond. He didn't want to hurt her, but he didn't want to mislead her either. Their time together was over. The sooner she accepted that, the better off they'd all be.

Chapter Five

Abby couldn't forget Noah's kiss.

She'd tried to put it out of her mind. But after his phone call, the memory played itself over and over in her head as she tried to sleep. She turned over, trying to find the cool side of the pillow for the thousandth time. After another thirty seconds she gave up. She sat up, yanked off the covers, and then reached over to snap on the light.

"This is ridiculous," she said to Annie, the rag doll her dad had gotten her when she was two.

From her perch on the dresser, Annie stared at her with faded blue eyes.

"I mean, it's not like I've never been kissed before," Abby continued when the doll offered no words of comfort. "But why did Noah kiss me? And why can't I stop thinking about it?"

She sighed and looked around her cozy bedroom as if the answer might be found in the soft, buttery yellow tones of the walls. Her gaze fell on a small framed wedding picture of her parents.

"Can you believe I'm going to marry him?" she asked in disbelief. "I hardly know him, Annie. What am I going to do?"

She swung her legs out of bed, reached over, and grabbed the still silent Annie from her perch. Abby hugged the doll to her chest.

"He's a nice guy and all. But not my type. He's not into commitment. He's not even into staying in one place. Only looking for a good time. Kind of like all the others, hey?"

She sighed again and snuggled back under the

covers with Annie's soft body in her arms. "Why did he kiss me? It's not like this marriage is for real. I mean, he doesn't think—"

She stopped in horror and sat bolt upright. Did Noah think they were going to have a real honeymoon even though the wedding wasn't real? At least not real for them. No, he couldn't be thinking that, could he? But then again, if he was like all the others, and they'd already established he was, that could be exactly what he expected.

Well, he was in for a surprise. He might be that kind of guy, but she was not that kind of girl.

She reached to turn out the light, then pulled the covers over her and Annie. With a determined effort, she closed her eyes and willed herself to fall asleep in order to escape the troubling thoughts tumbling through her mind.

The next few nights were no better, because as tired as she was, she could only control her thoughts while she was awake. Then she could prevent, with effort, thoughts of Noah and their upcoming wedding from intruding in her day. At night, when she was asleep and unconscious, her dreams replayed their kiss again and again. And as dreams are wont to do, they added things too.

She dreamed of the way Claire had kissed Noah at her apartment. But in the dream, it was Abby kissing him instead.

And they didn't stop with a kiss.

Abby woke with a start. Her heart rapped out a quick rhythm. Her breath came in quick gasps.

It took a moment for her to realize where she was. Sunlight streamed through the sheer curtains of her bedroom window. She turned over to make sure she was alone in the bed.

The dream had been so vivid.

She swore she could still feel the whisper of Noah's lips against her bare skin. Feel the weight of his body as he pinned her beneath him.

Would he want to do those things for real on their fake honeymoon?

A sick feeling of dread lodged in the pit of her stomach.

She'd had no contact with Noah since he'd been out of town. She couldn't decide if that was a good thing or a bad thing.

And she missed Claire.

They hadn't spoken since Claire had lied to her about having a date with Noah.

Abby grabbed the phone from the bedside table. She dialed Claire's number with shaking fingers. Would she answer this time? What would Claire say? Had *she* finally talked to Noah?

Part of her was annoyed with him for not returning Claire's calls. Getting the two of them back on track would go a long way in repairing Abby's friendship with Claire.

On the other hand, the thought of them going out again made her feel uneasy. She didn't want to imagine them together.

"Uh, hi, it's Abby," she managed to get out when Claire answered. But at least she'd picked up. Maybe she was ready to accept Abby's apology.

"Oh." Claire didn't sound too thrilled. "Hi."

Abby's hopes plummeted. "So, um, what's been going on? I feel like I haven't talked to you in ages." Mostly because Claire had been avoiding her calls. But Abby tried to keep the conversation casual.

"Yeah, I've been busy. Work and all."

Would Claire mention Noah? Say she'd seen him, even if she hadn't? Abby wouldn't let on that she knew Claire had lied to her before.

"Well, I wondered if—"

"I can't talk right now. I was just heading out."

Abby's heart froze. She sensed the lie through the phone. "Okay, well give me a call when you get the chance."

"Sure."

"Claire?" Abby rushed on before Claire hung up.

"What?"

"I really am sorry about..." she faltered. "About everything."

Silence stretched over the line.

"Are you still there?"

"Yeah, I'm still here."

"Did you hear what I said?" Abby asked.

"I heard you."

"I just wanted you to know." She'd said it a million times already. How many would it take before Claire believed her? Before Claire forgave her?

"Okay."

"I'll talk to you soon?"

"I really have to go." Claire hung up.

Abby clicked the phone off with a sigh.

She jumped when it rang again almost immediately. "Hello?"

"Abby Walker?"

"Yes."

"This is Sue over at the studio. I'm just checking in to see if you had any questions before leaving next week."

Next week. She swallowed the lump in her throat. "N...no, I think I'm all set."

"Great. I tried to give your fiancé a call, but only got his machine."

"He's out of town, but I think he's set too."

"Super. We'll see you on Monday then."

Abby clicked off the phone. She'd almost told the truth. One thing remained on her to-do list. She needed to buy a wedding dress.

She'd been putting it off. Buying one would make the charade even more real. But the time had come.

She chose a boutique far from her house. She didn't want to take the chance of running into someone she knew.

A petite saleswoman met her at the door. "May I help you, hon?"

"Um, yes, I need, that is I have to buy a, um, wedding dress."

"I'm sorry, we don't carry wedding dresses."

"No, it's not a real—I mean, I'm not looking for anything fancy. We're getting married," the word fell like a boulder in her stomach, "on the beach."

"Oh how romantic," the saleslady gushed. "I think we do have something that might be suitable. Follow me."

The woman showed her several dresses. Abby chose three to take into the dressing room. She slid into the first one, a simple white sheath with spaghetti straps. Tears sprang to her eyes as she looked in the mirror.

In her wildest dreams she'd never envisioned trying on wedding dresses in this way. Trying to hide. Afraid someone she knew would see her. A wedding should be a happy occasion. Not one she was ashamed of.

She took a deep breath and pushed the curtain aside. "Excuse me. Could you zip this for me?"

The saleswoman scurried over. "You look lovely."

"Thank you." Could the woman hear the tremor in her voice?

"When's the wedding?"

"Ne...next week."

"I bet you can hardly wait. Nothing's more wonderful than two hearts finding each other. True love is rare and special. Don't ever take it for granted." She smoothed the folds of the gown. "Your man is going to fall in love with you all over again when he sees you in this."

Abby bit her lip until she tasted blood.

"My George and I have been married for forty years. I love him more now than the day I married him."

An ache bloomed in Abby's chest. She'd been brought up to believe marriage was a sacred bond between two people who loved each other. Not something to be discarded after a week of fun and adventure.

Those words sent chills down her spine. She could almost imagine her grandmother rolling over in her grave. For the first time in her life, she was glad her parents were on the other side of the world.

"That's won...wonderful," she said in response to the woman's comment.

"I'm sure you and your man will have just as many wonderful years together." She looked at the gown on Abby again. "So, what do you think? Would you like to try on the other dresses?"

"No, I don't think so. This one is fine." She didn't care.

"Excellent." The woman unzipped the back of the dress. "As soon as you're ready, I'll ring you up."

"Thank you," Abby murmured, then fled into the dressing room.

****

The next few days passed much too quickly. If she could have found a way to slow down time, or stop it entirely, she would have done it. Even if it meant throwing the rest of the cosmos into indescribable chaos.

But time marched on, and the day of the wedding arrived.

Her dress hung in a garment bag on the back of her door. Everything else was in her suitcase, ready to go. Before zipping the lid closed, she grabbed Annie from the dresser and laid her on top of the clothes.

She glanced around the room. The next time she'd see it she'd be a married woman waiting for a divorce. No, not a divorce, an annulment. The technical correction didn't make her feel any better. Never in a million years had she ever imagined herself doing something like this. Make that a billion.

She dragged her things to the living room, her heart as heavy as her suitcase. After checking the house one final time for any appliances or lights she might have left on, she sat down to wait for the limousine that would take her to the airport.

She didn't have long to dwell on her upcoming marriage. The doorbell pealed.

Taking a fortifying breath, she pulled open the door.

"Noah." Surprise tinged her voice. She'd expected the driver.

"Hi."

"Hi." She took in his presence. He, of course, looked the same, except he seemed tanner than he had before. He'd been someplace warm. And he had faint, bruise-like smudges under his eyes. Apparently he hadn't been sleeping well either. Whether from stress about their situation or entertaining the ladies wherever he'd been, she didn't want to know.

"Are you ready?" Noah broke the silence after he, too, had studied her.

"As ready as I'll ever be," Abby said. "I need to get my things."

"Let me give you a hand." Noah grabbed her suitcase and the garment bag.

"It's not a bad day out," he commented as they made their way to the curb and the waiting car. After passing her things to the driver, who stowed them in the trunk, they climbed into the spacious back seat.

"No, it's nice today."

"It should be even nicer in Key West. I checked it out online last night. It's going to be perfect."

Abby gritted her teeth at the inane pleasantries. Were they really talking about the weather?

Silence fell. That was worse than the weather talk. She jumped when Noah spoke.

"Did you get the message from the studio about the film crew?"

She nodded. From the time they arrived at the airport, they would be taped for the show.

"I think we should play it up a little, you know?"

"What?"

"I mean, I think—" Noah cleared his throat. "We should act like we're happy about this. You know, pretend we're excited about getting married."

Her heart beat a painful rhythm in her chest as memories of her troubled dreams rushed back to her. What did he expect her to do?

"I think it would look bad if we didn't at least seem excited about all of this. After all, we're supposed to be getting married because we want to."

"So," she found her voice at last, "what are you suggesting?" Even to her own ears she sounded apprehensive.

"Nothing major," Noah assured her. "Just, you know, hold hands and stuff when the cameras are on us."

"Oh." That didn't sound too bad. After all, she didn't want to be one of those women who found their husbands on some reality show, then got ripped apart in the tabloids for it. Of course this situation was different. Those women had gone on TV *looking* for a husband. As far as anyone knew, she and Noah had only been on TV looking for a *wedding*.

The distinction didn't make her feel any better, but Noah did have a point. They might as well play the charade to the fullest. "Okay."

Is that why Noah had kissed her the other day? No, it couldn't be. There hadn't been any cameras around then. She had to let it go before she drove herself crazy.

All too soon they arrived at the airport. The driver came around to open their door.

"Show time." Noah gave her a reassuring smile, then exited the limousine ahead of her. He turned to assist her out. A small camera crew documented their arrival. Noah kept hold of her hand as he led her into the terminal. Abby ignored how right his touch felt, and smiled and waved. Did she look as sick as she felt?

They passed through security, then found their seats in the first class section of the plane. In deference to other passengers aboard, they wouldn't be filmed during the flight.

After breakfast, Abby settled into her seat. Hoping to avoid anymore meaningless small talk, she closed her eyes and pretended to sleep.

****

Noah studied Abby as she feigned sleep next to him. Although reluctant to admit it, he'd missed her while he'd been away.

The kiss he never should have stolen haunted him. Why had he done it? Other than it had seemed like the right thing to do at the time.

He wasn't used to second guessing his motives. Kissing beautiful women wasn't anything new, but somehow it had been different with Abby. Thoughts of her had prevented him from enjoying the company of several willing females on his latest trip. He'd felt as if he'd been cheating on her by talking to them.

He still imagined he could feel her lips moving softly beneath his own. And taste her sweet breath as it mingled with his.

His body stirred at the memory. He shifted in

his seat.

It would be best to get this farce of a marriage over with, so he could get on with his life. The thought of being married sat like a heavy weight on his shoulders. He wasn't about to fall into the trap that had ensnared his parents.

The sooner this ended, the better.

Because maybe then he could forget how right it felt when Abby drifted off to sleep for real and snuggled into the curve of his shoulder.

****

Abby awoke from her nap cuddled against Noah. Her head rested on his shoulder, his arm warm and secure around her. The steady beat of his heart pulsed beneath her ear and she sighed in contentment, shifting even closer to the heat of his body.

"Hey, sleepyhead, we're almost there."

The deep voice close to her other ear jolted her fully awake. Why was she draped across Noah? She pulled away, pushing the hair back from her face. She blinked sleep from her eyes.

"Uh, sorry," she stammered. A flush of heat crept into her cheeks. "I...I guess I fell asleep." Nothing like stating the obvious.

"No problem." His voice sounded a little strained.

"Did you say we were almost there?" she asked to change the subject.

"Yeah. We'll be landing in about half an hour."

"Oh." Her heart doubled its rhythm. Once they landed it wouldn't be long before they were married. And then they'd be off on their honeymoon. Doubts assailed her, and a familiar troupe of butterflies danced in her stomach. How far would Noah want to take their charade?

"You okay?" He covered her hand with his own where it lay on the armrest between them.

No, she wanted to shout. However, she smiled in what she hoped was a reassuring manner. "Sure. I mean, hey, the sooner this gets started the sooner it will be over, right?"

"Right."

They disembarked from the plane. Her legs shook. Her heart drummed. She clung to Noah's hand like a lifeline as they made their way past the Florida based camera crew, offering a plastered-on smile and half-hearted wave.

A limousine whisked them to their hotel. At last she had a moment to herself.

She unpacked a few items. She took Annie out of the suitcase and set her on the dresser. Then Abby sat down on the bed and looked at the rag doll.

"What am I doing, Annie? This isn't me. I can't be getting ready to marry a man I hardly know. How did this all happen?"

Annie had no words of comfort to offer, so Abby got up to change into the dress she would wear for her wedding. Her fingers fumbled with the zipper. Her trembling hands smoothed down the skirt of the gown. The simple sheath was nothing like the Scarlett O'Hara gown she'd often envisioned, but perhaps that was for the best.

After she had dressed, a representative from the show arrived to do her hair and makeup. A limousine drove her to the ceremony. Could the driver hear the painful thumping of her heart through the glass partition that separated them?

Another car had been sent for Noah. She hadn't seen him since they'd arrived at the hotel.

She smiled and waved at the ever-present cameras as she alighted from the luxurious sedan. Was this how celebrities felt? Always having to look as if they were enjoying themselves in public. If this was what it was like to be famous, she didn't want any part of it.

Dari, the wedding coordinator, escorted her to the bridal room. Abby sat on the flower-patterned bench along one wall and closed her eyes. She leaned her head against the pink floral wallpaper.

"May I come in?"

She opened her eyes. Noah's head poked around the edge of the door.

"Sure." She rose to face him as he stepped into the room. Her eyes swept down his tall frame. He wore a black suit, and his tan appeared deeper above the collar of the crisp white of his dress shirt. A grey silk tie was knotted around his neck, and a small red rosebud was tucked into the buttonhole on the lapel.

He looked gorgeous.

And calm.

Her stomach churned. Her legs trembled. Her heart sped.

"Are you okay?"

Abby laughed, surprising herself. She didn't think she'd find anything to laugh about considering their current situation. But he had greeted her with similar words so often over the last several weeks that she had to smile.

"As okay as I'm going to get." She might as well be honest.

"You look beautiful." His gaze swept over her. "You're the most beautiful bride I've ever seen."

Abby staggered under the weight of his words. One word in particular. Bride. She was the bride. Tears welled in her eyes.

Noah must have noticed the betraying moisture. He crossed to her and took her cold hands in his. "It's going to be all right."

"How? I can't believe I'm the bride. Of all the ways I've ever imagined this day, never in a million years would I have pictured it like this."

"I know. I wish there'd been some way to—"

She pulled her hand from his and placed a

finger over his lips to stop his words. The movement of his mouth felt like a kiss against her skin. She pushed the thought away.

"Don't," she said. "We've been over this too many times. There was nothing we could do."

Noah didn't reply, but took her hand and placed a kiss in the center of the palm. Her pulse skittered over the spot, then raced into overtime at the emotion burning in his eyes.

He cupped her face in his hands, drawing her upward as he lowered his head. He brushed his lips over hers.

"You're amazing," he whispered.

"Wh...what?" Abby couldn't control the trembling in her limbs, which increased the moment his lips touched hers.

"I have something for you." Noah moved away and reached into the inside pocket of his suit. He pulled out an elongated jeweler's box and handed it to her.

"What is it?"

Noah smiled, sending a rush of warmth through her. "Well, I've always heard that a bride should have something old, something new, something borrowed, and something blue." His gaze swept over her dress. "I figured you had the new part covered. This should take care of everything else. Open it," he prompted when she hesitated.

She tore her gaze from the sweet intensity of his, then opened the box. Inside, nestled on a bed of soft velvet, lay a blue porcelain pendant suspended from a delicate gold chain.

She gasped. "It's beautiful."

Noah took the box from her shaking fingers and removed the necklace. "Turn around."

She complied. He slipped the chain around her neck. The soft touch of his fingers at her nape as he fastened it raised goose bumps on her flesh.

"It belonged to my great-grandmother." Noah turned her to face him once again. He adjusted the pendant. His knuckles brushed her skin above the top of her dress. She shivered.

"I know this isn't the dream wedding you've always imagined," he continued, "but I wanted you to wear this. All of the Grant brides have worn it on their wedding days."

"But I'm not really—"

This time Noah placed a gentle finger on her lips to stop her words. "It doesn't matter. You've been so great through all of this, and I wanted to tell you how much I admire you."

"Are you kidding? I've wanted to throw up on a regular basis for the last month."

He chuckled. "Yeah, me too." He adjusted the necklace once more, sending tremors through her at the touch of his skin against hers. "It looks perfect on you."

The tremors turned to trembling as Noah gazed down at her. She looked up into his eyes. The intent in them was clear.

His head lowered, and, without conscious thought on her part, she raised her lips to his.

His mouth brushed over hers. Once, twice, before he deepened the kiss. She melted into the heat of his mouth. Why was it, out of all the craziness of the last few weeks, the only sane place seemed to be in Noah's arms at this moment? With his mouth stroking over hers with sweet force. It didn't make any sense.

A knock sounded at the door, and the wedding coordinator entered without waiting for a reply.

"Can't wait until after the wedding, huh? What a pair of lovebirds."

Noah broke the kiss, and a guilty blush crept into Abby's cheeks. She avoided looking at him as she ran a hand over her hair to smooth it.

"Are you two set?"

She nodded, unable to speak as Noah replied, "Sure." His voice held a husky note that hadn't been there before.

The coordinator handed Abby a fragrant bouquet of red roses, which she took with shaking hands.

"All right, let's get you two married."

Chapter Six

The beach at sunset. A setting any bride would fantasize about. Waves lapped at the shore. The warm Gulf breeze rustled the ivy and magnolia twined around the arbor arching overhead. Their sweet fragrance filled the air.

Abby clutched the bouquet of roses, unable to appreciate the beauty of her surroundings. She stood, surrounded by a camera crew instead of the family and friends she would have imagined at such an occasion, facing Noah. If she could keep her eyes fixed on a steady point, her world had a chance of not spinning out of control as it threatened to do. So she kept her gaze glued to his face.

As if in a dream, she heard herself say the required "I do" at the appropriate place and Noah's echo a few seconds later. Although how the words made it past the huge lump in her throat, she would never know. Noah slid a ring on her finger, and someone handed her another one to slip on his. She glanced at the matching gold bands. Hers looked out of place on her finger. Then the justice of the peace pronounced them husband and wife.

They were married. 'Til death do us part. Or until the annulment next week. A touch of hysteria crept into her mind.

"You may kiss the bride."

She snapped back to the present as the words registered.

The kiss was brief, but sweet, a brush of his lips across hers before he raised his head and smiled down at her. Without meaning to, she smiled back at him, then looked around, startled, when the camera crew broke into applause.

"Congratulations," the wedding coordinator gushed. "Now, we'd like to get some still pictures, and then we'll send you on your way for tonight. Tomorrow's a busy day, don't forget," she continued as Abby and Noah obediently posed for pictures.

Abby thought her face might crack from smiling so much. Purple blobs floated in front of her eyes from all the flashes. She blinked.

"Okay, that should do it. The car is here whenever you're ready to head back to the hotel."

Abby followed the coordinator across the beach, but Noah's tug on her hand stopped her.

"We'll be there in a minute."

She turned questioning eyes to him.

"Want to go for a walk on the beach?"

"Now?"

"Sure, why not? Come on," he said. "It's a shame to waste this beautiful night." He led her toward the edge of the water, then bent to remove his shoes and socks and roll up the legs of his pants. Following his example Abby kicked off her shoes, leaving them in a careless pile next to his, and gathered the bottom of her dress in one hand. Noah took her other hand and they headed down the beach. They left footprints in the damp sand. The water lapped at their feet with the ebb and flow of the waves.

They walked in silence. The soothing sound of the water washed over her. The sun grazed the horizon, bathing the entire beach in a warm, orange glow. It reminded her of a scene from a movie. A fairytale, some would say. But the man walking by her side holding her hand was all too real.

Her husband.

The word, applied to Noah, seemed almost as unreal as the thought of princes and princesses and enchanted castles.

Noah broke the silence and into her thoughts. "What are you thinking?"

She shrugged. "Probably the same thing you are." She looked over at him and offered a smile, which he returned.

"So, if this had been your real wedding, what would have been different?"

The question surprised her. It disheartened her when not one single image came to mind. For the life of her, she couldn't come up with any other way she would wish her wedding to be, other than standing on the beach at sunset with Noah. She didn't have an answer for him.

"We, uh, we really should be heading back," she said instead. "It's getting dark."

Noah's gaze searched hers, then he nodded. "Sure, if that's what you want to do."

"It's been a long day. I'm pretty wiped out." Abby would never admit, even under threat of torture, that all she wanted to do was stay out on the beach with Noah. Perhaps even for eternity. The safe thing to do, the *sane* thing to do, was head back to the hotel and get some much needed sleep.

Weariness weighed her down and slowed her steps on the way back up the beach to the waiting limousine. She was almost too tired on the drive to worry about the sleeping arrangements for the night. Almost. A tight knot clutched her stomach by the time they reached the door of their suite.

Noah seemed to sense her discomfort, because as soon as they entered the room, he tossed his coat, which he'd carried over his shoulder, on the couch in the sitting room. He dropped down on the cushions. "I'll grab a pillow and a blanket from the closet and sleep here."

She nodded and let out the breath she'd been holding. She ignored the tiny stab of disappointment that pricked at her from a secret place deep inside.

"Well," she found her voice at last, "I guess I'll turn in for the night."

"Yeah, me too. Sounds as if we have a big day of sightseeing ahead of us."

On the way back to the hotel a representative from the show had briefed them on their schedule for the next day. A camera crew would follow them around Key West as they began the first stage of their "honeymoon." Later that night they'd board the cruise ship that would take them on the rest of their trip.

"Okay, good night then." What a strange thing to say to her new husband.

"Good night."

Abby walked into the adjoining bedroom. She closed and locked the door behind her. Her gaze fell on the bottle of champagne chilling in a bucket on the nightstand beside the king-sized bed. Two crystal flutes, engraved with the words *Bride* and *Groom*, stood nearby. She hesitated. Did Noah want a drink? She could do with one herself.

She'd almost reached the adjoining door, in fact her hand had reached for the knob, before she changed her mind. Instead she headed into the bathroom to change out of her dress. She managed to get the zipper only a couple of inches down before it stuck. She tried pulling it back up, but it wouldn't budge.

"Darn it."

After struggling with it for a few more minutes, she gave up. The dress was too tight to come off without unzipping it. "I guess I'll have to sleep in the dang thing," she muttered.

She bit her lip. She could ask Noah for help. But asking him to help her out of her wedding dress brought to mind connotations she didn't want to think about.

She'd sleep in it.

She took off her makeup, brushed her teeth, then slid under the covers. It took all of ten seconds to realize how uncomfortable sleeping in the dress would be.

She swung her legs over the side of the bed and stood. After staring at the door separating her from Noah for a full five minutes, she decided she was being ridiculous. She needed help with a stubborn zipper. No big deal. He wouldn't be undressing her.

She unlocked the door with trembling fingers, then stopped. She shouldn't barge in. So she knocked and called through the door. "Noah?" Was he already asleep?

But he answered right away. "Just a minute."

She stood, gnawing her bottom lip, until the door opened. Her gaze slid over him. He wore the pants from his suit. And nothing else. With an effort born of Hercules himself, she avoided staring at his bare chest.

"Is something wrong?"

"N...no. I, um, the zipper of my dress is stuck." She stepped into the sitting room.

An unreadable expression crossed Noah's face. "Oh."

"Can you, I mean, would you help me please?" She turned and presented her back.

She sensed him hesitate. Then. "Uh, sure." Maybe he had been sleeping, because his voice sounded husky.

His breath whispered across her bare shoulders as he moved closer. He tugged at the back of her dress. "The fabric's caught," he explained. "There." Cool air touched her back. His fingers brushed her spine as he lowered the zipper.

Shivers raced across her body, raising goose pimples in their wake. She sucked in her breath.

Behind her, Noah cleared his throat. "All set." Long seconds passed before he removed his hands, then stepped away.

She almost turned to face him, then thought the better of it. "Th...thanks." She fled into the safety of her own room, shutting the door behind her.

****

Noah stared at the closed door. He tried not to think about it not being locked. Abby had locked it the first time. He'd heard the telltale click earlier. But not this time.

He closed his eyes, picturing how she had looked on the beach with the soft glow of the sunset around her. And how she'd looked after he'd kissed her before the wedding. And how she had looked just now with the vulnerable nape of her neck exposed as she held her hair out of the way. Her bare skin smooth and soft against his fingers as he'd lowered the zipper, revealing the gentle curve of her spine.

Then he imagined how she'd look as he slid the dress down, leaving her bare. As he drew her into his arms. As he kissed her again. As he made love to her.

He took a step toward the door, then froze. What was he doing? What was he *thinking*? About Abby. She wasn't some girl he'd met in the course of his travels. She was his wife.

His temporary wife.

Making love to her would make their marriage all too real.

He couldn't go down that path. Things were too complicated already. He only hoped by the time this was all over she wouldn't hate him too much. She'd looked so scared when she'd stepped into his room. As if she'd been afraid he was going to jump on her.

Here he was contemplating doing that very thing. As he'd done with countless other women over the years.

It wouldn't be like that with Abby, he argued with himself. It would be different. He didn't know why. But the thought scared the hell out of him.

Throwing himself onto the couch, he sighed. He closed his eyes, but images of Abby continued to taunt him. He wasn't going to sleep. Not with his mind on Abby and his body aroused. He stood to remove the pants he had donned when Abby had called to him. He stripped down to his, somewhat, more comfortable boxers.

Back on the couch he tried to find a position to ease his discomfort, but fought a losing battle. He recited the alphabet backward. Tonight it would take him about a zillion times through to ease the ache of wanting Abby.

****

Abby awoke the next morning, surprised she'd fallen asleep at all. She showered, then dressed in a simple, flowered sundress. A knock on the door made her jump. Her pulse accelerated. What would she say to her new husband in the light of day?

"Abby?"

"Yes?" she called through the door, not afraid to open the door and face Noah, but not eager to open it either.

"Breakfast is here. Are you hungry?"

At the mention of food, her stomach growled. "I'll be right there."

Taking a deep breath, she walked into the sitting room. Noah wore khaki shorts and a wild Hawaiian shirt. A fact she was grateful for.

"Good morning."

"Good morning." She sat at the round table laden with a variety of breakfast items. Delectable pastries were artfully arranged on a china plate. A bowl of exotic fruit sat to one side of a vase overflowing with fresh flowers. Tall, tapered candles glowed with a soft, flickering light. A silver platter of eggs and bacon sat in the center. A napkin folded into the shape of a swan graced each place setting.

Everything looked so romantic. Perfect for a honeymoon.

She swallowed.

"Juice?" Noah indicated the crystal carafe.

"Yes, please." Great. Back to inane pleasantries.

They ate in silence. The quiet grated on her nerves. Someone had to say something.

"Have you ever been to Key West before?"

Noah swallowed the bite he'd been chewing. "Nope. I have to admit, I'm looking forward to some of the sightseeing. I hear the shipwreck museum is one of the best."

"I can't wait to see Hemingway's house. Can you believe all those cats really live there?"

"They're supposed to all be descendents of Hemingway's own cats. In fact, they've been inbred for so long most of them have six toes."

She looked at him askance. "Really?"

Noah shrugged. "It's what I've heard."

She gave a mock shudder. "That's too weird."

"Weird, but true."

They chatted about other places they wanted to visit on the island, until a knock on the door interrupted their solitude.

Noah rose to answer it, then stepped back to admit the representative from the TV show they'd met the day before.

"Whenever you two are ready, the film crew's all set outside. We'll do a couple hours of filming and then give you some time alone."

"A couple of hours?"

"Well, we need to get as much footage as we can so we're able to piece together the best of it for the show," the man explained. "I'll send the makeup and hair people up if that's okay?"

"Sure that's fine."

In no time at all, the stylist had arranged Abby's hair in a clip at the back of her head, leaving a few loose tendrils to curl around her face, then applied her makeup.

"Do you feel like a movie star?" Noah teased.

"Not quite, rock star," she replied with a smile as Noah received a quick dusting of powder.

He grabbed his camera before they headed out the door.

Despite the presence of the show's crew and Noah's insistence she pose for pictures for him from time to time as well, Abby enjoyed herself. After the cold, blustery winds of Chicago, the warm, moist Gulf breeze felt like heaven. They explored the Shipwreck Historeum and the Key West Aquarium with the film crew trailing behind. At first all of the attention they attracted unsettled her, but after a while she almost forgot she and Noah weren't alone. A trip out to the Southernmost Point in the Continental U.S. on the touristy Conch Train completed their time with the crew, who then waved good-bye, saying they'd see them later on the ship.

"Hungry?" Noah asked.

She nodded. "Sure."

They made their way to the famous Sloppy Joes. After ordering, she sat back and looked at Noah.

"Okay, so I never thought I'd be saying this..."

"But?"

"I'm having fun today."

Noah laughed.

But her words were true. She was in an amazing place, with beautiful weather and incredible things to see and do. She wasn't paying for a thing. The company wasn't bad either, especially now that they had ditched the camera crew.

Noah proved to be an appealing traveling companion. He had read up on some of the places they'd visited and added tidbits to the guides' monologues. And he was funny. He'd had her laughing more than once as he'd regaled her with tales about his other travels.

"I'd say 'I told you so', but that wouldn't be very gentlemanlike of me," Noah responded.

She stuck her tongue out at him.

"Hey. That's something my seven-year-old nieces would do."

She laughed at his wounded expression, then became serious. "Tell me about your family."

"Like what?"

"Oh, I don't know. Anything."

"All right, let me introduce them to you." Noah pulled his wallet from his back pocket.

She averted her gaze from the upward flex of his hips as he did so.

He set a series of pictures out on the table between them. "This is my sister Barbie and her husband Tom. Zoe is seven, Fiona is three, and Amelia just turned one." He pointed to the next picture. "This is my sister Angela and her husband Eric. Meg is seven, Jenna is four, and Erin is their newest. Then I have two brothers. Jeremy is married to Michelle, and they have Tay, who's four, and Alli. My brother Matt recently got married, and he and his wife Lisa have Rachel."

Noah grinned. "And that's it for now. Although I'm sure Barbie won't be content with three kids for too long."

"Wow," Abby said. "That's quite a crew."

"Yeah, you should be around at the holidays."

"What are your brothers and sisters like? Are they all adventurous like you?"

Noah smiled at her slight emphasis on the word *adventurous*. "No, they're definitely not that. For the most part, they're content to stay at home and add to the Grant family tree."

"And you?"

"That's not the life for me. I don't want any part of something like that."

She pushed aside a stab of disappointment. He sounded so determined. So final.

But she couldn't stop herself from asking. "Not ever?"

Noah shrugged. "It's not me. I'd hate to be tied down to a family and not be able to be spontaneous."

"Oh."

"I watched my parents live a life like that because of me."

"Because of you?"

"My mom was pregnant, so they had to get married." Noah said the words matter of factly, but she could tell it bothered him. "Then after they had me, they kept having more kids. They were stuck."

"Oh." She didn't know what else to say. To her, Noah's life sounded like heaven on Earth. Brothers and sisters to play with. Staying put in one place. His view on it puzzled her.

"Were your parents unhappy?"

Noah looked startled at the question. "Heck no," he replied. "Don't get me wrong. They were—they are—perfectly content with their life. They love each other more than any other couple I know. We still catch them making out all the time."

"Really?" The revelation shocked Abby. Being an old-fashioned military couple, her parents never even held hands in public.

"Yeah, it's usually when they're supposed to be doing the dishes after Thanksgiving or Christmas dinner."

"And your brothers and sisters?"

"Pretty much the same. As you can see"—he swept his hand over the pictures still lined up on the table—"all happily married, making babies one right after the other."

She frowned. Noah seemed so different from the rest of his family, but then again, perhaps it was that black sheep thing. She didn't understand how he could feel the way he did. She would have given anything to have a life like he'd had growing up. She wanted a life like that now.

But she hadn't found anyone to settle down with. No one worthy of sharing her grand plan. The world was full of too many men who wanted a quick fling with no strings attached. Men who barely let the sheets cool before moving on to the next bed.

Men like Noah.

"Hemingway's next?" he asked, interrupting the unfavorable line of her thoughts.

Abby agreed, but recalling their conversation that morning, decided to avoid all cats, six-toed or not, while they were there.

If Noah brushed against her while they waited in line, or held her hand even when the camera crew wasn't there, well that was expected. A habit more than anything. That's all. She wasn't about to become another notch in his bedpost, so she might as well enjoy his company and the situation the best she could. She wouldn't let his attitude about life rain on her sunny day.

But of course, the clouds were inevitable. The dark spot came while they were shopping at a small outdoor market. Abby browsed the crowded aisles, and Noah spent most of his time talking to the very blond, very leggy girl behind the cash register. She should have expected it. She'd always heard people say "every cloud has a silver lining." Except for her, the opposite held true, like "into your life a little rain must fall." Even on beautiful, sunny days in Key West.

She averted her eyes as Noah bent his head close to the girl's while they were deep in conversation. And she pretended not to see when the girl slid something into his hand which he slipped into his shirt pocket.

Was Noah collecting phone numbers on their

honeymoon? Not that the honeymoon was real, but they had gotten married less than twenty-four hours ago. Then again, that wasn't real either. Still, shouldn't he have a little more respect than that?

She shook her head to clear the tangle of thoughts.

"All set?"

Apparently he was done flirting.

"Yes, I'm set. Are *you* done?"

Noah frowned at the tone of her voice, which even she had to admit sounded snotty. "I'm done." He looked at his watch. "We really should be heading back. I have to repack some things before I'm ready to head to the ship."

"Okay."

They ambled toward their hotel. For the first time all day Abby didn't know what to say.

He nudged her with his arm. "You're quiet all of a sudden."

"I'm tired I guess."

"Would you rather take the trolley?"

"No, walking is fine."

They continued in silence, until Noah spoke again. "Is something wrong?"

She didn't look at him. "No." She wouldn't play the role of jealous wife. They hadn't made a real commitment to each other. Noah could flirt with whoever he wanted. She had no right to be upset. But she did wish he had at least waited until their fake honeymoon was over.

When she raised her hand to brush a loose strand of hair out of her eyes, the gold band on her finger glinted mockingly at her in the afternoon sun. She set her jaw and ignored the curious glances Noah threw her way.

After what seemed like an eternity, they at last made it back to the hotel, and Abby was able to escape to the sanctuary of the bedroom to pack. She had zipped her suitcase, with Annie riding shotgun on top of all the clothes, when Noah poked his head into the room.

"Can I talk to you for a minute?"

She couldn't refuse. What was she going to do, hide in the bathroom?

"Sure," she said without much enthusiasm.

"I just wanted to—" Noah cut himself off. "Abby, have I done something wrong?"

Did she need to spell it out for him? Well, forget it, she wasn't going to play that game. "Why do you say that?"

He crossed the room to stand in front of her. She fought the urge to take a step back.

"Well, I thought that in spite of everything, we were having a good time today."

She nodded. She had been having a good time. Right up until bleached blondie with the never-ending legs.

Before she could say anything, Noah rushed on. "You've seemed distant since we left that marketplace." He grabbed her hand and pulled her down to sit next to him on the edge of the bed. "I know the last few weeks haven't been easy for you. But I wanted to tell you again how much I admire you. So, I, uh, I wanted to give you this."

He reached into his shirt pocket and produced a small, flat package.

"You...you bought me something?" A lump lodged in her throat.

She stared at the object in his hand. Is that what he had slipped into his pocket earlier? A present for her?

"Yeah, this reminded me of you. Of us." He opened the folded paper to reveal a delicate silver bracelet. The links were etched with intertwining ivy.

"You shouldn't have." She didn't know what else

to say.

"I wanted to. Here, let me put it on you." He lifted her right hand and fastened the chain around her wrist. "There." He paused for a moment before continuing. "My sister-in-law is really into symbolism and all that stuff, and I remembered her saying that ivy was a symbol of memories and friendship and affection. I figured that was appropriate."

He smiled at her, and her pulse quickened. "I don't know what to say. I love it. Thank you."

"You're welcome."

"You didn't need to buy me anything."

"Like I said, I wanted to. Besides," he winked, "I got a great deal on it. I had to haggle with the clerk, but she finally gave in."

"Is that what you were talking to her about?" Shock crashed through her.

"I was trying to keep it a secret, but you kept looking over at us." Noah stopped. "What did you think I was doing?"

Abby lowered her eyes, not wanting him to see the guilt in them. "I thought...well, I thought that you—"

"You thought I was hitting on her."

It wasn't a question. The flat tone of Noah's voice sent a shiver down her spine. She had misjudged him.

"I'm sorry. I—"

"Do you really have that low an opinion of me?"

The combination of hurt and anger in his voice chipped at her heart. She put her hand on his arm. "No, I don't."

"Yes, you do." His look accused her. "We just got married. How could you think I'd do that to you?"

"But we're not married. I mean, it's not real."

"I know, I know." Noah threaded his fingers through his hair, his frustration evident. "I can't believe you thought..." His words trailed off.

"I really am sorry." Her mind whirled. Her thoughts tangled. The Noah she'd spent the last couple of days with wasn't anything like the man she'd imagined him to be. The man he'd claimed to be. Who was the real Noah?

She didn't have time to ponder the question, because he took both her hands in his, drawing her attention back to him. "Know this. While we're married. For this week, this trip, this asinine show, I am committed to you." He paused and raised one hand to tuck a wisp of hair behind her ear. "Totally. Completely. Committed. To you." With each word his voice and head lowered, until the last was a whisper against her lips.

Chapter Seven

Noah's hand slid around to the back of her neck, then up into her hair, unfastening the clip and tossing it aside. He tangled his fingers in the strands that fell free and held her close as he deepened the kiss.

Abby wrapped her arms around him as the tip of his tongue teased the fullness of her bottom lip. When she opened to him and he dipped inside, she almost melted from the flood of liquid heat that suffused her body. Warmth spread to her limbs and made her pliant as, his mouth never leaving hers, Noah lowered them both to the bed.

He slid a hand around her shoulder and down her arm to rest at her waist. He fanned his fingers out, the tips brushing the underside of her breast. Although he didn't move his hand again, the sweet threat of it hung suspended around them.

His kiss was deep. And possessive, as if sealing the vow he had spoken only moments ago.

Or was it hours? The insistent pressure of Noah's mouth left her dazed and unable to form a coherent thought.

The ringing of the phone nearly didn't penetrate the sensual fog. But when it rang again, she jerked away from him.

"Dammit." He rolled away and reached for the phone. "Yes?" His tone was curt, raspy.

She sat up and gulped air into her lungs as if she'd been drowning. Which wasn't far from the truth.

Noah hung up the phone. "The..." He cleared his

throat. "The car will be here in a half hour."

She nodded, not trusting her voice. Noah lay prone on the bed. He looked tempting. And aroused. She tore her gaze away from his shorts and stared at a spot on the wall in front of her.

He wanted her.

What would have happened if the phone hadn't rung? And what would happen tonight when they were alone in their cabin on the ship? Would he expect to pick up where they'd left off?

Would she?

Abby wrapped her arms around herself, chilled, yet still warm. Too warm.

Behind her on the bed, Noah muttered under his breath. Finally, with what sounded like, "see, bee, ay," he inhaled a big gulp of air, then slowly let it back out. He sat up.

She didn't look at him. They sat in silence until after what seemed like a millennium, Noah cleared his throat again.

"I guess I should finish packing." His voice held a husky note, but sounded steady.

"I'm about ready." Abby's voice wasn't quite as steady, but at least the words made it out.

After another long pause, Noah stood. "Okay, let me know when you're through, and I'll help you with your things."

She nodded. Noah left the room and closed the door behind him. She exhaled the breath she'd been holding. She grabbed Annie from the suitcase and collapsed back on the bed.

She hugged the doll to her and squeezed her eyes shut. What was happening to her? She'd gone from being angry to confused to aroused in such a short span of time that her head still spun. Not to mention the erratic pace of her pounding heart.

"Annie, what am I doing?" she whispered. She opened her eyes to stare at the ceiling. "I'm the one who keeps saying this isn't a real honeymoon, but the first chance I got I fell into bed with him. Or at least *onto* the bed with him. Why does he affect me like this?"

She could count her entire dating history on the fingers of one hand. She'd dated in high school, in whatever part of the world she'd been in at the time, and she'd had a serious boyfriend in college. But when Abby thought they were at the point of making a commitment and settling down, he'd been offered a job overseas and decided he needed to see the world before making any plans for the future.

Since then, she'd had a handful of relationships here and there, but no one had wanted to share her dream of settling down. At first she'd thought the men she'd dated had wanted the same things as she did, but all had turned out to be dead ends. Most men were only interested in one thing.

The same thing Noah seemed to be interested in.

But that wasn't what bothered Abby. What bothered her was *her* interest in *him*. She couldn't ever remember anyone making her feel the way Noah did. At times she only had to look at him, and she went weak in the knees.

Which was bad.

She wasn't the kind of girl to jump into bed with a guy for the sheer pleasure of it. She needed something more. For her, sex was the continuation of a relationship, not the whole reason for it.

A relationship with Noah was out of the question. For a multitude of reasons.

Not the least being, he wasn't interested in one.

"So, Annie, that's that. All Noah will ever be is my husband for a week.

Annie, as usual, made no reply to the ridiculous statement, so Abby gave her one last squeeze and rose from the bed.

She placed the doll on the pile of clothes in her suitcase and, with a whispered "I'll see you later," zipped the luggage closed.

A soft knock on the door made Abby jump. Heat suffused her face as Noah appeared in the doorway.

"You all set?"

She nodded, thankful when he didn't mention the kiss. Then again, what was there to say? She was more than happy to pretend the whole thing had never happened.

"Just these?" He indicated her suitcase and garment bag.

"Yeah, that's it. I can grab this." She took the bag from him as she spoke, ignoring the jolt of awareness that speared through her when his fingers brushed hers. So much for pretending.

They walked down to the car, then rode in silence to the dock where they would board their cruise ship. At the sight of the huge vessel, her stomach clenched. She had to spend a week on the ship with Noah. On a honeymoon that was beginning to sound dangerously enticing.

Abby pushed the thought aside. She wasn't that kind of girl.

After they left their luggage with a porter, the representative from the game show greeted them. "We'd like to get some footage of you two boarding the ship. Then we'll film again later on deck as we leave port."

They headed up the ramp leading to an open hatchway in the side of the massive ship. Noah took her hand. Tiny shocks of awareness shot through her. She ignored them.

Holding hands was all part of the game. They'd gotten carried away before. It wouldn't happen again. She wouldn't let it happen again.

The cameras panned to follow them, a reminder of how much of a game it was. She and Noah waved and smiled.

"How much footage of us waving can they possibly need?" she muttered under her breath.

Noah smiled down at her. "Oh, about three thousand hours should do it."

She laughed up at him, breaking some of the tension left from their encounter at the hotel. Funny Noah she could handle. Sexy, kissing her until she was senseless Noah was a different story.

"Okay folks, that should do it for now. We'll need you back on deck when we sail, but for now you're on your own."

Noah thanked the cameraman, then turned to her. He glanced at his watch. "We have some time before we can get into our cabin. What are you up for?"

"I don't know. What are our options? You're the world traveler here, you can be the tour guide. My expertise is limited to military bases."

"I'm not going to be much of a tour guide. I've never been on a cruise before."

"Really? You mean there's something Mr. Adventurous actually hasn't done before?" Abby teased.

"Very funny."

They strolled along the deck. Her heels clicked on the boards. "I figured a cruise would be right up your alley. You get to see a whole lot of things all on one trip."

Noah shrugged. "Too scheduled. They tell you when to eat, when to go exploring. I'd rather make those decisions on my own."

"So all of this TV show stuff must really be driving you crazy. They have everything planned almost to the minute."

"Yeah, it's more structured than I usually prefer, but, hell, it's a free vacation. I can't really complain. What about you?"

"What about me?"

"Are you a structure girl or a live-by-the-seat-of-your-pants girl?"

She laughed. "What do you think?"

Noah looked down at her, his smile answering hers. "Yeah, that's what I kind of figured. Are you enjoying any of this?" His hand swept out, taking in the vast expanse of ship around them.

"I really am having fun," she admitted. As long as they weren't having too much fun. The wrong kind of fun that had seemed so right back at the hotel. "And like you said, I can't complain about a free vacation."

"What about the being married part?"

The question surprised her. "I'm trying not to think about that part."

He raised an eyebrow, but didn't comment. "You hungry?"

"I could go for a bite to eat."

He stopped near a hatchway to examine a map posted on the wall. "I think if we head that way," he pointed, "we should find the à la carte restaurant."

"Sounds good to me."

They made their way into the interior of the massive ship.

Abby admired the luxury surrounding her. Deep, plush burgundy carpet cushioned her feet in the corridors. The walls were paneled in dark, rich wood. Polished brass railings gleamed, reflecting the light from the crystal chandeliers that dangled overhead. In the main lobby, glass elevators took passengers to the many decks soaring above the marble floors.

They found the restaurant at last. Passengers crowded the spacious area.

"Wow, I guess everyone had the same idea we did," she said with a laugh.

"I guess so. Well, let's get something to eat.

Maybe by the time we've made it through the line, a table will open up."

"Sounds like a plan."

They chatted while they waited, and the line moved quickly. They were looking for a place to sit when Abby noticed a little boy about four years old. He had tears streaming down his face. His eyes darted around the room.

She halted Noah's progress by grabbing his arm. "Oh, Noah, look." She pointed to the small boy. "I wonder if he's lost."

"Poor little guy, he looks scared to death. Here." He handed her his sandwich. "I'll be right back."

Noah approached the crying boy and crouched in front of him. At first the child looked more afraid than before, but as Noah spoke to him, his tears subsided. Soon he nodded, then wiped his eyes and nose on the sleeve of his shirt. When Noah rose and held out his hand, the boy took it.

The pair approached Abby.

Her imagination took flight. What would it feel like to be married to Noah for real, and for him to be leading their son toward her? Maybe they'd be expecting their next one, doing their part to add to the Grant family tree.

She blinked to push the disturbing image away. Where had those thoughts come from?

"You were right. This little guy seems to have gotten separated from his parents. Do you think you could find someone to page them? I'll stay here with him in case his mom and dad come back."

"Sure." She turned to the little boy. "What's your name, sweetie?"

"Danny," the boy told her. "I was looking at the fishies." He pointed to a large aquarium on the other side of the room.

"They're fun to look at aren't they?" She turned to Noah. "I'll be back as soon as I can."

"We'll be here. Thank you." His smile melted her heart.

She hurried off and explained the situation to the first uniformed crew member she found. The man promised to page the boy's parents and send them to the à la carte restaurant.

On her way back to Noah and the boy, the announcement came over the loudspeaker. Upon entering the restaurant, she found them looking at the fish tank. Before she could greet them, a frantic looking couple rushed into the room.

"Danny!" the woman exclaimed.

"Mommy! Daddy!" The boy raced into their outstretched arms.

They held him for a moment, then turned to Abby and Noah. "Thank you so much." The woman paused, swallowing, then continued. "This has never happened before. I thought he was with Jim, and Jim thought he was with me. We..." Her eyes filled with tears.

Her husband put his arm around her. "Honey, it's okay. Everything turned out fine thanks to these folks." He turned to Abby and Noah once again. "Really, we can't thank you enough."

Noah put his arm around Abby's shoulders, mirroring the other man's gesture. "We're glad we could help."

"Danny, don't ever wander away from Mommy and Daddy again."

"I was looking at the fishies." The little boy pointed at the large aquarium again. "Then you went away." His lower lip trembled. "You leaved me all alone."

"I know, baby." His mother held him close. "Can you say thank you to the nice man and his wife?"

"Thank you, nice man," Danny repeated.

A flush crept into Abby's cheeks at being referred to as Noah's wife, but the boy's words made her smile.

As the rest of the adults laughed, Noah hunkered down in front of the child. "No problem, buddy. Stick close to Mommy and Dad, okay?"

"Okay." Danny slapped his small hand against Noah's raised one.

"Do you have children?" the woman asked after Noah rose to his feet.

"Uh, no, we're uh, on our honeymoon." Noah darted a quick look at Abby.

Was it her imagination that he looked a little green?

"Well, congratulations. And thank you again. You'll make a wonderful father some day."

As the reunited family walked away, Abby snuck a look at Noah. He had definitely paled beneath his tan.

She ignored the woman's comment and changed the subject. "We should probably eat these." She indicated the sandwiches in her hand.

"What? Oh, yeah, that's probably a good idea." Noah shook his head, as if to clear it. He still looked uncomfortable.

They found an open table and ate in silence.

Finally, having slaked her hunger, she studied Noah. "I don't understand you."

"What do you mean? I'm an open book."

"Yeah, right." She laughed in spite of herself. "You say you don't like kids, but you were so great with that little boy."

"I never said I don't like kids. I adore my nieces. I just don't want any of my own."

"You keep saying that. Why not?"

"I just don't okay?" Noah's voice was curt. "It's not a big deal. Can we drop it please?"

"Sure." A little taken back by Noah's tone, she sat in silence. She hadn't meant to offend him. Even if she didn't understand his point of view, it wasn't her place to judge him. She didn't know him well enough to do that. Even as his wife for the week.

"Hey." Noah broke into her thoughts. He reached for her hand across the table and twined his fingers with hers. "I'm sorry. I didn't mean to snap at you."

"It's all right. I shouldn't have said anything. It's none of my business."

"No, it's not that. I—" Noah stopped and ran the fingers of his other hand through his hair. "Look, it's not a subject I like to discuss, that's all."

"Okay. I can live with that."

"It really isn't a big deal."

"Noah, it's fine. We don't have to talk about it." Even as Abby assured him, it piqued her curiosity more than ever. What made Noah so adamant about not wanting to have kids? Did it have to do with his wanderlust? Or was there more to it than that?

As curious as she was, it shouldn't concern her, so she made a determined effort to put it out of her mind.

They chatted about inconsequential things until an announcement over the loudspeaker proclaimed the ship would be sailing within the hour. Visitors needed to go ashore. She and Noah finished their makeshift meal, then headed out to the boat deck, where they met the film crew.

The television station had made special arrangements to use the bow of the massive ship for filming, so she and Noah posed for pictures and were filmed as the ship sailed out of port and into the Gulf of Mexico.

With his arms wrapped around her from behind, her back pressed to his chest, he inclined his head to whisper in her ear. "Feeling like a movie star again? Hopefully this ship won't sink."

She turned to laugh up at him.

Unprompted by the film crew, he dropped a kiss

on her lips.

Cameras flashed around them.

"Thanks, you two. We're good for today. We'll get more footage tomorrow in Cozumel. Your cabin should be ready by now. Have a nice evening."

"Thanks. You too."

On their own, she and Noah strolled hand in hand through the elegant corridors of the cruise ship. The scent of wood polish and fresh flowers permeated the air. Contentment settled over her.

The porter opened the door to their cabin and ushered them inside.

Her contentment vanished, replaced by a lump in her throat. She swallowed. The lump settled in her stomach. A shiver of apprehension—or was it something else?—flowed down her spine.

A king-sized bed dominated the small room.

And there wasn't a couch in sight.

Chapter Eight

"Are you okay in there?" Noah's voice filtered through the bathroom door.

"I'm fine. I...I'll be right out." Abby took a deep breath and looked at herself in the tiny mirror above the small sink. She'd been hiding out in the bathroom for a while now. No wonder Noah sounded concerned.

After a nice dinner, aside from a rather embarrassing rendition of "Happy Honeymoon to You" by the wait staff, she and Noah had explored the ship further. They strolled the decks around the two pool areas, peeked into several of the nightclubs, and found many shops and boutiques in the mini mall on one of the main decks. They even tried their hand at some slot machines in the casino.

The ship oozed elegance and luxury, but she wasn't able to appreciate any of it. She kept picturing the bed that took up most of the space in their tiny cabin.

The tiny cabin they'd need to share for the next week.

What would happen? If the weak-kneed feeling of being in Noah's arms earlier hadn't been so fresh, maybe she wouldn't have dwelt on it so much. But she could swear her lips still tasted his kiss and her breasts still tingled from his near touch. Even now, she watched her face in the mirror flood with color at the sensual memory.

She couldn't stay in the bathroom all week. She had to face the situation, and Noah, sooner or later. It may as well be sooner.

With a final fortifying breath, she slid open the door and walked out into the cabin she'd share with her husband for the next five days. Noah sat propped up against the headboard of the massive bed, flipping through channels on the TV suspended in one corner of the room.

He greeted her with a smile. "I thought you fell in."

She tried, but couldn't quite match his teasing grin. "Sorry, did you need to get in?" She hovered near the door.

"No, I wanted to make sure you were okay." Noah flicked off the television and contemplated her.

She fought the urge to peek down to make sure she was covered, even though her T-shirt and shorts were far from revealing. She didn't want to give him any ideas, although judging by earlier, he had ideas of his own anyway.

"Did you want to watch some TV?" Noah asked, when the silence had stretched too far to be comfortable.

She shrugged.

"What's wrong?"

"Nothing."

Noah shot her a puzzled look. "Are you sure you feel okay?"

She nodded.

"Abby."

She gave in to the compelling tone of his voice. He sounded genuinely concerned. "There's no couch."

"What?"

"Where are we going to sleep?" There, she'd come right out and said it.

Comprehension dawned in his eyes. "Is that what you're worried about?"

She nodded.

"Well, then stop worrying. I'll grab a pillow and a blanket and sleep on the floor."

She shook her head. "There's no room."

"I'll be fine. There's plenty of room here next to the balcony door."

The space he'd indicated didn't look big enough to accommodate his tall frame.

Reading her still skeptical expression, Noah laughed. "Really. It'll be fine. I've slept in much smaller spaces."

"Why don't you take the bed? I'll take the floor. You're bigger than me."

Now Noah shook his head. "Nope. That wouldn't be very gentlemanly of me." He reached across the bed and grabbed her hand. "C'mon, sit with me and watch some TV. Or are you going to stand there all night? I guess it would solve the sleeping problem, but I don't think you'll be very comfortable."

His tone teased, but she resisted the slight tug on her wrist.

"I'll stay on my side, I promise." Noah made a crossing motion over his heart. "Come on," he repeated, when she still hesitated. "I'll even keep one foot on the floor, like in the old movies."

Abby drifted toward the bed. "What?"

"You know, in the old movies in any of the bedroom scenes, the actors needed to keep one foot on the floor at all times. To keep things all nice and proper."

"Is that really true?" She inched closer.

"It's what I've heard. That's my girl." Noah smiled as she sat down on the edge of the bed. "What do you want to watch?"

"Doesn't matter. I'll probably fall asleep anyway, I'm beat."

"Yeah, I'm getting there. It's been a busy day."

Noah flipped channels for a while as they watched whatever caught their interest for a moment or two.

"Is there anything specific you wanted to do in

Cozumel tomorrow? Other than what the television show people have planned." He grinned and waved a parade queen wave while he waggled his eyebrows.

Abby laughed. "I've heard the shopping is great, but I'm sure that won't be interesting for you."

"I could shop for a while. I think I read that you can rent scooters and tool around."

"That might be fun." She grabbed a sheaf of papers from the nightstand and glanced at their itinerary for the next day. "We're not in port for very long."

"Sounds like a plan then." Noah aimed the remote at the television one last time and flicked off the set. "Well, I think I'm going to turn in." He grabbed a pillow from the bed and a blanket from the closet. He arranged himself on the floor.

She peeked over the side of the bed. Noah could barely stretch out in the small space. "Are you sure about this?"

"I'm sure." He sat up, bringing his face close to hers.

She made herself stay still, even though her first instinct was to pull back. Was he going to kiss her again? And if he did would she be able to stop herself from inviting him to share the bed with her? Because that was her greatest fear. Not that Noah would want to sleep with her, but that she wouldn't be strong enough to say *no* if he asked.

His lips grazed her forehead. "Now, turn off the light. I'm wiped out."

She complied, then snuggled down under the covers of the cozy, oversized bed. On the floor, Noah rustled around. In the soft moonlight filtering in from between the blinds of the balcony door, she saw him sit up and pull his shirt over his head.

She flipped over. Would he take his shorts off too?

She lay awake for a long while, sensing Noah

hadn't fallen asleep either. Was he uncomfortable? Should she say something? Should she invite him to share the bed, for sleeping, in the literal sense? Maybe they could do that foot on the floor thing he'd mentioned earlier.

Or maybe she should stop thinking about him and try to get some sleep.

****

Abby wasn't asleep yet. Noah could hear her restless movements in the bed. He tried not to think about her in that big bed. Alone.

He'd spooked her back in the hotel on Key West. He'd gone too far. He'd only been thinking about how good she felt in his arms. How sweet she tasted and how soft her skin was.

He felt like a cad, but at the same time he wanted nothing more than to finish what they'd started. But she'd looked so scared, so vulnerable, as she stood outside the bathroom earlier, as if she were waiting for him to pounce on her.

It had taken a lot of willpower not to do that very thing. She was beautiful and sweet and wonderful and adorable.

And she was his wife.

At least for a while.

He admired how she was handling the situation. She was way out of her comfort zone, but she was being a trouper as they played through their farce of a marriage.

He didn't want to have anything to do with commitment or marriage or babies or anything related to that, but when he looked at Abby all he wanted to do was take her in his arms and make her his wife for real, consummating their marriage. Although that seemed like such a cold word for all of the delicious, erotic, warm, sexy things he wanted to do with her.

If it were anyone else, he wouldn't be sleeping

on the floor alone tonight. He knew what women wanted and what they liked. Most were eager to fall into his arms and into his bed.

The women he went out with knew, as much as he did, that it was all for fun. No commitments, no questions, no complications. They were all grown ups, playing grown-up games with rules that everyone understood.

Abby was different. Almost as much as he wanted her, he wanted to protect her.

It galled him that what she needed protection from most was him. He wanted her.

And that scared the hell out of him.

So he vowed not to kiss her anymore. Kissing her only made him want to do other things with her. Things that he had no right to think about.

Because Abby was his wife.

The usual rules didn't apply.

****

Abby awoke to another sunny day, this one in Cozumel, Mexico. Noah didn't look any worse the wear from sleeping on the floor all night. In fact, he looked decidedly sexy in a rumpled, morning kind of way.

"Do you want the shower first?" she asked.

"No, you go ahead." Noah rose from the jumble of blankets on the floor. He stretched, then ran a hand down his tanned, bare chest.

Her gaze followed the movement, then lingered at the top of his shorts, where a thin trail of dark hair disappeared into the low-riding waistband.

"Abby?"

She yanked her gaze away. Heat suffused her face. She swallowed. "What?"

Noah looked bemused. "I said you go ahead with the shower. I'm going to sit out on the balcony for a while."

"Oh, right. Sure. I won't be long." She grabbed

clothes for the day, then fled into the safety of the bathroom.

Taking a shower in the tiny stall was no mean feat, and after banging her elbow on the wall for the fifteenth time, she swore. Why was everything on the ship so blasted small?

"Everything except the colossal, giant, humongous bed in the middle of the room," she grumbled as she emerged from the bathroom.

"Did you say something?" Noah came through the balcony door.

"No. Nothing. What's that?" She gestured to the paper in his hand.

"Oh, the TV people dropped this by while you were in the shower. Apparently we're giving interviews today."

"Interviews? What do you mean?"

Noah shrugged, drawing her attention to his chest once again. He'd pulled a shirt on, but hadn't buttoned it, and the effect was almost more devastating than his bare chest had been. He looked as if he'd stepped right off the cover of *Stud Weekly*.

"Abby?"

For the second time in less than an hour, she jerked her attention away from a place it shouldn't have been in the first place. "What?"

"You haven't heard a word I've said all morning. What's wrong with you?"

"Nothing." Only trying to reign in her inappropriately raging hormones. "I'm sorry. What were you saying? Something about interviews?"

Noah handed her the sheet of paper. "Here. Take a look. They're going to interview each of us separately to find out how we feel about each other."

Her heart stuttered. "How we feel about each other?" Now there was a question she didn't even want to begin to explore. How *did* she feel about Noah?

"You know, all that mushy stuff about how we met and why we fell in love, and how we're soul mates and don't know how we managed to live until we found each other." Noah headed into the bathroom.

"Excuse me?"

"Come on, Abby." His voice came to her through the open door. "You've seen all those reality shows where they interview each person in a separate room to create some tension and drama."

"I don't think—" she began.

"It'll be fun." Noah poked his head around the doorway. Shaving cream covered the lower half of his face, but a wicked gleam lit his eyes. "We'll lie."

Before she could retort, or hit him for using the word *fun* again, he closed the door. His cheerful whistle filtered through the thin barrier. She guessed lying wasn't something that bothered Noah Grant.

She plopped down on the bed and stared at the ceiling. Then again, everything *she'd* done in her life since she'd met him had been one huge, continuous, never-ending lie. What difference would one more make?

When he emerged from the bathroom fifteen minutes later, his shirt on and buttoned, she rolled to face him.

"Okay." Abby propped her head up on her hand.

"Okay what?"

"We need to get our stories straight. If we're going to have all this fun lying, we'd better do it right."

"That's my girl." Noah grinned and sat on the edge of the bed. The mattress dipped from his weight. She shifted before her body touched his. His aftershave tickled her nostrils.

"What do you have in mind?" he asked.

"Well, I think we should be sure we're telling

them the same thing. If I say we met in Chicago, and you say we met in San Francisco, they might get suspicious."

"Makes sense."

"Well, you probably have more experience lying than I do, so any suggestions?"

"Hey." Noah looked hurt. "What's that supposed to mean?"

"Nothing. Really," she added when his expression didn't change. She laid her hand on his arm where it rested on his bent knee. "We need a plan."

Noah regarded her for another moment, then nodded. "Right. Well, in my *experience*"—he shot her a wry look—"the closer you stay to the truth the less chance you have of slipping up."

"Good. So, we met in Chicago."

"Yeah, and a mutual friend set us up." Noah used her words from all those weeks ago on the game show when everything had started to go wrong.

Abby smiled, but then it turned into a frown. "Claire." She sighed and changed her position on the bed, sitting up against the headboard. "She hates me."

"Why would she hate you? I thought you guys were pretty close."

"We were. Before all of this." She swept her hand out to encompass the cabin. "Before you." Her gaze met his for a brief moment before darting away.

"Hey." Noah used a finger to turn her face back to him. "Claire's the one who asked you to take her place on that game show. You were doing her a favor, remember?"

"And am I still doing her a favor by being here on a honeymoon with her boyfriend?"

"Look," Noah said, the words clipped. "I told you before. I'm not Claire's boyfriend. She's someone I met at a bar and went out with a couple of times. We had a good time together. Nothing serious. If Claire thought so, she had the wrong idea. We never made a commitment to each other."

The words were meant to reassure, but instead they made Abby wonder how many countless other girls he had met at a bar and had a good time with. Or on one of his trips. Or at the corner coffeehouse. Or anywhere.

"No," she said in response to his last statement. "You're not committed to anyone, or anything except having fun." Her gaze fell to her wrist and the bracelet he'd bought her the day before. The words he'd said when he'd given it to her leapt into her mind. He'd said he was committed to her for this trip. Another lie. The words had sounded so sincere, because they were what she had wanted to hear. But Noah didn't know the first thing about commitment. He'd made it more than clear he didn't want to know.

"Look, Claire's a big girl. I'm sure she'll be fine."

"Yeah." She'd almost forgotten they'd been talking about Claire. Claire *would* be all right. Eventually.

Their friendship might not be, and Abby wasn't sure if *she'd* ever be okay again. She had the feeling all of this—Noah—was going to change her life forever. Nothing would ever be the same.

"So, what else do we need to be sure we're on the same page about?"

She gave herself a mental shake and turned her focus back to the topic of their original conversation. "I don't know. How long have we been together?"

"Does that matter?"

"Well, if they ask, you can't say one thing and me another. So, how long?"

He shrugged. "I don't know. A year?"

"And we're getting married already?"

"Too soon? How long would you want to know a guy before getting married?"

"A few years or so. I'd need to date him for at least a year, then have about a year to plan the wedding after we got engaged."

"It takes a year to plan a wedding?" Noah sounded aghast.

"If you want to do it right. Real life isn't like TV-land here. You have to think about the church, the reception hall, the flowers, the cake, the dresses, the—"

"Okay, okay, I get it. There's a lot of stuff to think about."

"So, how long have we been together then?"

"You seem to have the timetable in your head. You tell me."

She glared. "Three years."

"Fine, three years."

"How did you propose?"

"What?"

"This is a wedding show. They're going to want to know how you proposed." Frustration crept into her voice.

"At a basketball game on the big screen?"

She shot him a dirty look.

He held up a hand. "Whoa, easy there. Okay, no basketball game. Did I get down on one knee?"

"Definitely. And there were flowers. Where were we?"

"A restaurant?"

"Too public."

He sighed and ran his fingers through his hair. "A candlelit dinner at your place?"

"Perfect. What about—"

Noah interrupted. "Look, as long as we don't get too specific about details, we should be fine. Keep your comments as general as possible."

"I guess." Still not satisfied, but knowing she

wouldn't get anything else out of Mr. Fly-by-the-Seat-of-His-Pants, she scooted off the bed.

Noah grabbed her arm. "You don't have a very high opinion of me, do you?" He'd asked her something similar before.

"I'm not sure I know you well enough to have any kind of opinion about you." What she did know about him confused her. All she wanted to do was make it through the rest of the cruise and chalk the whole thing up to a really bizarre experience. To do that, she needed to put some distance between herself and Noah.

He wasn't good for her. By his own words he was the kind of guy she'd never in a million years even think about dating.

And she'd married him.

Time for some breathing room.

"I need to finish getting ready." She moved toward the opposite edge of the bed.

This time Noah let her go.

Chapter Nine

Abby and Noah met with the representative from the game show at a designated spot on the waterfront.

Try as she might, Abby couldn't enjoy the spectacular view. Her stomach somersaulted at the thought of the questions she'd be asked and the lies she'd need to tell.

A glance at Noah revealed that he looked calm, as usual. The upcoming ordeal didn't seem to be causing him any anxiety. At times like this, as much as it often irritated her, she wished she shared his carefree outlook on life.

"We'd like to do the interviews separately, if you don't mind. Who wants to go first?"

Noah turned to her. "Why don't you start? I'll grab a drink somewhere." He looked at his watch. "How long will this take?"

The game show representative shrugged. "Not more than half an hour."

"Great." He kissed Abby on the cheek, then brushed his thumb over the spot. His gaze lingered on hers a moment.

She wanted to look away, but something compelled her to keep her eyes locked with his. So much for her vow to put a little breathing space between them.

"I'll meet you back here in a little bit. Have fun." He waggled his eyebrows at her before sauntering away.

She watched him go. The easy swagger of his hips caused a funny flip in her tummy.

"You found a good one there."

"What?" Abby jerked her attention back to the other woman.

"Your husband," she continued. "I've seen a lot of couples on this show. But there's something different about the two of you."

Abby's breath caught. Had their secret been discovered? "Wha-what do you mean?"

"I'm not sure. Something about the way he looks at you. It's like the way he feels about you is right there for everyone to see." She shrugged. "I'd be willing to bet that most of the marriages generated from this show don't last very long. But you two, I can tell you're in it for the long haul."

Abby bit her lip to keep the hysterical bubble of laughter from escaping. What would the woman say if she knew they'd made plans to end their marriage even before it began? And what could she possibly be seeing on Noah's face?

"Sorry to go on like that," the woman said. "It's just the romantic in me. Anyway, let's have you take a seat right here." She gestured to one of the tall studio chairs set up in front of the breathtaking view of crystal blue sky and sea. A large sculpture of intertwining vines arched overhead. In the background, on the water, their cruise ship lay at anchor. The entire tableau faced a simple set up of cameras and lights.

"This is one of the most popular picture spots here in Cozumel," the woman explained while makeup people touched up Abby's face and hair. "We thought it would be perfect for the interviews."

"Is this where you always do them?" Abby asked.

"No, actually we've never done interviews before. This is a whole new format for the show. Usually we don't film anything beyond the game show itself. But the producers wanted something special to celebrate the hundredth episode, so they decided to incorporate the wedding and a weeklong trip into a follow up show. Normally the prize for the winning couple is just a private weekend getaway wedding somewhere. Vegas or Reno or someplace like that. You guys were really lucky."

"Yeah. Lucky." Abby resisted the urge to roll her eyes. "So, uh, why the interviews?"

"It makes it more personal. We figured people wouldn't want to watch a show where you simply get married. We wanted to show the love story behind the wedding."

"Oh. Great," Abby murmured with a polite, albeit false, smile. It would be a story all right.

A man came over to clip a microphone onto the neckline of her sundress.

"Okay, I think we're set. Here's how this will work. Sandy is going to ask you some questions. Answer them with whatever comes to mind. There aren't any right or wrong answers. We just want our viewers to have the chance to get to know you and Noah a little bit."

Abby nodded. She smoothed her clammy hands down her thighs. She'd gone over possible questions and answers in her mind a thousand times. Everything would be fine. She pulled a deep gulp of air into her lungs, then slowly exhaled.

A woman with perfectly coiffed blond hair settled herself into the other chair. She held out her hand. "Hi, I'm Sandy."

"Abby."

"Nice to meet you." Sandy glanced at the note cards in her hand, then up at the man behind the camera. "Ready?"

"We're rolling."

"Great." She turned to Abby. "How did you and Noah meet?"

Abby breathed a silent sigh of relief. They'd practiced that one. They were off to a good start with the questions.

"A mutual friend introduced us." Her relief faded as her answer made her think of Claire. Would Claire still be her friend when all of this was over? Was Claire still her friend now? The way things had been in the weeks leading up to the wedding, Abby didn't think so. Once everything was over and done with, and she and Noah were divorced, would Claire be willing to talk to her again? Could Abby finally make her understand that everything had been one giant mix up from the very beginning?

Would Noah go back to dating Claire?

The thought caused a lump to form in Abby's throat. She hadn't thought about that before.

But it made sense. Noah and Claire would probably pick up right where they'd left off. Abby recalled the way Claire had kissed Noah the day they'd broken the news of their impending marriage to her.

Obviously Claire was interested in continuing her relationship with Noah.

How did Noah feel about that? He insisted that what he and Claire had wasn't anything serious. But did he really mean it? Was he only saying that for Abby's sake?

Somehow she didn't think so.

So, what would happen when they returned?

"Abby?"

Abby jumped. Her attention snapped back to the woman at her side. "I'm sorry, what?"

"You were a million miles away." Sandy smiled. "Maybe that answers my question."

Abby blushed. "I...I'm sorry, I didn't hear you."

"So I gathered. What I wanted to know is if it was love at first sight for you and Noah?"

"I don't know about love at first sight, but I definitely liked Noah from the moment I met him." That was true. He had made the whole game show and wedding mess much easier to deal with. His constant calm and reassurance were like a lifeline. Her harbor in the storm.

"How long had you two known each other before you knew you would marry Noah?"

Abby suppressed a smile and allowed herself to relax. The predictable questions were almost laughable. Were people really interested in hearing this kind of stuff? "It wasn't long after I'd met Noah that I knew I'd be married to him someday." About two hours to be exact. She hid another small smile at her private joke.

"How did you know he was the one?"

Abby bit her lip. That one was harder. "I...I don't know if I can explain it. It's not really something I can put into words. I just *knew*." Her answer sounded lame even to her own ears. She winced. She'd read dozens of romance novels, but for the life of her she couldn't remember how any of the characters described love. What love felt like. Could love even be described? Wasn't it just a feeling?

It's not like harps played and lightning flashed in real life. The earth didn't move.

Except when Noah kissed her.

Except when his arms wrapped around her, holding her close to his hard strength.

Except when the heat flowed from his body to hers.

Except when—

Sandy cleared her throat.

Abby blinked and shook her head to clear the images from her mind. "What? Sorry, I don't know what's wrong with me today."

Sandy smiled, a knowing look on her face. "Don't worry about it. We'll edit out the long pauses." She nodded in the direction Noah had gone. "I wouldn't be able to stay focused if I had a husband like that either. Obviously you're very much in love. So, on that note, what are the things you love best about Noah?"

Abby shifted in her chair. The questions were far more personal than she'd anticipated.

It made her uncomfortable to think about loving Noah.

What would the audience want to hear? "He's kind and caring. He's close to his family." That was the truth. And if she *were* in love with someone, those would be the things she'd want him to be. She thought about Noah sleeping on the floor last night. "He's selfless. He puts other people's needs before his own."

The words sounded good. Exactly what a woman in love with her husband would say. But were they true? Sure, Noah had been overly gracious about the sleeping arrangement the previous couple of nights, but he really did seem to be more of an *all-about-me* kind of person. After all he didn't want to get married and have a family of his own because of the restrictions it would place on him.

That wasn't very selfless. In fact, that was pretty self-centered. Not at all the kind of person she'd ever fall in love with for real.

Which was fine, since she wasn't in love with him for real. Only for pretend.

So did it really matter what she said?

Not in the least.

"A sunset wedding and a cruise ship honeymoon are very romantic. Is Noah romantic in other ways?"

Abby hesitated. Was Noah the romantic type? She couldn't quite imagine it, but she couldn't say that.

For some reason it made her feel odd to think about him being romantic. As if it were too personal.

Which was ridiculous. How could anything be more personal than being married to him? Than trying to describe what it felt like to love him?

Trying to stall, she smoothed her hands over her dress again. The silver bracelet caught her eye.

"Yes, he's very romantic." Why not? she decided. The viewers wouldn't want to hear that he wasn't. "He's always surprising me with little gifts." The bracelet reminded her of another piece of jewelry he'd given her. "On our wedding day he gave me a pendant that belonged to his great grandmother. In his family, it's a tradition that all brides wear it."

The kiss they'd shared afterward popped into her mind. Talk about romantic. And the kiss after he'd given her the bracelet. It had started out romantic. Then it had turned sensual and bone melting and utterly devastating to her senses. She blushed again.

"So, what happens after the honeymoon"

Abby forced her wandering mind back to Sandy. Again. "I...I'm sorry, what?" How many times had she apologized for not paying attention. She was going to look and sound like an absolute moron when this part of the show aired.

Sandy smiled. "What will life be like for you two after you get back home?"

"I guess things will go back to normal. All of this," she gestured to the water and the ship behind them, "has been like something out of a fantasy." Or a nightmare, depending on the perspective.

"No big plans to start a family anytime soon?"

"No, no. Nothing like that." Not for Noah at least. Someday Abby wanted a family. But it wouldn't be with him.

Strange. Someday she'd be married to someone else. But it seemed odd to think of having another wedding. Another husband. Would she refer to Noah as her ex-husband? Or would she simply pretend that none of this had ever happened?

After several more fairly predictable questions, Sandy turned to Abby with a smile. "Well, that should about do it. Thanks so much."

"You're welcome." Abby unclipped her microphone and handed it to the technician. She breathed a sigh of relief. It hadn't been the best half hour of her life, but it hadn't been the worst either.

"When your husband gets back we'll interview him, and then you two will be on your own for the rest of the day."

"Great."

As if on cue, Noah approached.

Sandy cast an appreciative glance at him. She looked over at Abby. "Do you thank your friend everyday for introducing the two of you? I bet you're glad she didn't want to keep him for herself."

Abby's heart dropped into her shoes. Claire *had* wanted to keep him for herself.

She swallowed. "Yeah, I'm really lucky." The words were barely a whisper.

What a sad predicament. In another week, not only would she not have Noah, but more than likely Claire would never speak to her again. Abby would never know what the future held for either of them. Would Claire and Noah be together?

If they didn't become a couple, would it be Abby's fault? Could they have made it work if Abby hadn't come into the picture?

Would Claire and Noah have won the game show? Would they be one of those couples that didn't work out? Or would theirs be a lasting relationship? Did they still have a chance?

She jumped when Noah put his arm around her shoulders. She looked up at him.

Something in her expression must have given her away.

He leaned down to whisper in her ear. "Was it that bad?"

At least he had no idea what she'd really been thinking. "No, it was fine." Without making it seem obvious, she stepped away from him, hoping the physical distance would alleviate the emotional guilt. "I'm sure you'll have just as much *fun*."

He grinned down at her. "I'm sure I will.

While Noah gave his interview, Abby found a bench a little distance away and gazed out over the water.

What a mess she'd gotten herself into. She couldn't quite wrap her head around the fact that she was married. To Noah. And they were on a honeymoon.

She lifted her face to the sky, letting the warmth of the sun caress her face. If nothing else, she had to admit that the weather was perfect. Temperatures in the mid-eighties and sun all the time were a far cry from the blustery cold winter winds of Chicago this time of year.

Thinking of Chicago made her think of Claire.

Not a far jump. Her thoughts had been on her friend all day.

What was she doing right now? She'd be at work most likely. Was she thinking about Abby? About the fact that Abby was on a honeymoon with Noah?

Did she think they were having a real honeymoon?

Yesterday the honeymoon had come dangerously close to being real.

How was Abby going to find a way to make things right with Claire? Convince her that nothing had happened between her and Noah. When something had.

Could she look her friend in the eye and lie?

Lying during an interview she didn't care about was far different than keeping the truth from her best friend.

If she had a best friend anymore. Things weren't looking good on that front.

"Penny for your thoughts."

Abby jumped at Noah's words. "You startled me."

"Sorry." He sat down on the bench next to her. "You okay?"

She drew in a deep breath to calm her racing heart. "Yeah. Fine. I didn't see you."

"Lost in thought?"

She offered a half smile. "Something like that."

He looked down at her, a thoughtful expression on his face. He nudged her with his arm. "I heard you said some nice things about me in your interview."

She tensed. What had Sandy told him? He had to know that everything was a lie, didn't he? "Oh, yeah?" she asked, hoping her voice sounded calm.

"Yeah." He didn't elaborate.

She strove for a casual tone. "Well, I had fun." She grinned up at him. "I lied."

For a moment he looked dumbfounded. Then a smile quirked his lips. "Nice."

"How did your interview go?"

"It was fine. Nothing surprising. Since you prepped me and all," he teased. He glanced at his watch. "What do you want to do next? We still have a couple hours in port."

"Window shopping? Or is that too girlie for you?"

"Oh, I think I can handle it." He took her hand as they strolled down the street.

Habit? Or had Sandy told him something Abby never would have wanted him to hear?

She shook off the paranoia. Whatever Sandy had said, Noah knew it was all part of the game. He wouldn't believe any of it.

"Did you really have fun in your interview?" Noah asked after they'd walked in silence for a while.

She glanced up at him. "Sure. It was okay. Why?"

"You seemed," he paused as if searching for the right word, "uncomfortable afterwards."

She looked away from his probing gaze. "I was thinking about Claire." Might as well be honest. She'd done enough lying for the day.

"Claire?" He sounded surprised.

On the pretense of brushing a strand of hair away from her face, she pulled her hand from his.

"Something Sandy said after the interview was over," she explained.

"You need to stop beating yourself up about Claire." Frustration tinged his words.

"Easy for you to say. Claire wants to talk to *you*." She couldn't keep the bitterness out of her voice.

"Why did you do it?"

She frowned. "What?"

"The whole game show thing. Why did you agree to take Claire's place?"

"Claire was desperate. She was really looking forward to the whole thing and then she sprained her ankle. I had to help her out, it meant a lot to her. Of course, I never dreamed I'd wind up winning. That I'd be here with you like this."

He smiled, as if enjoying a private joke.

The thought annoyed her. "What's so funny?" she snapped.

"Nothing." He composed his features. "Winning aside, something like that game show, it doesn't seem like you."

She shook her head with a rueful smile. "It isn't."

"Then back to my original question. Why did you do it?"

She sighed. "Claire is, well, was, my best friend, and—"

"*Is*," Noah interrupted.

She ignored him. "And she's always been there

for me. I wanted to help her out this time."

"By getting involved in this?" His hand swept out.

"You know how I told you we moved around a lot while I was growing up?" Why was she telling him this?

He nodded.

"I never had a best friend. I never had time to build lasting friendships at all. When I moved to Chicago, I met Claire. For the first time in my life, I had someone in it I wasn't going to have to say good-bye to in a couple of months or a year.

"We hit it off right away. And we've been friends ever since." A wistful sigh escaped. "Until now."

"Stop it."

The angry tone of Noah's voice took her by surprise. "What?"

"Stop taking the blame for all of this. Claire doesn't seem as if she's being a very good friend right now. Not if she won't even talk to you."

"No, no. You don't know her the way I do. Claire is wonderful. We have such a good time when we're together. We've laughed and cried over so many things together. When my grandma died she was the one who was there for me. She never left my side." She grimaced. "That's why when she asked me to do her a favor, I said *yes* right away. Being on a stupid game show for her was the least I could do." She looked up at the man walking at her side. "She did it for you, you know."

"For me?"

"She thought you'd be bummed if you didn't get to do it. She said you were really excited about it."

He snorted. "Right."

"She likes you a lot," Abby insisted. "This whole thing has been really hard on her.

Noah ignored that. "Harder than it's been on you?"

117

Abby lifted her chin. "Maybe."

He lifted an eyebrow, his skepticism apparent. "Oh, really?"

"Like you said, we're on a great vacation, we're not paying for a thing, the weather's amazing, but Claire's at home right now wondering what we're doing on our honeymoon. It has to be driving her crazy."

"Yeah, well we're not doing anything."

"I know." Abby ignored the memory of his lips against her own. Of his body pressed to hers. "But Claire doesn't know that."

"Because she won't listen to you. It drives me crazy that you keep defending her. She doesn't seem like a very good friend if she's mad about something as trivial as this."

"Trivial?" She couldn't believe what she was hearing. "Getting married is trivial?"

"In this case, yes. This isn't a real marriage, Abby."

"I know that," she bit out from between clenched teeth.

They walked in stony silence.

Finally Noah spoke. "I'm sorry." He guided her over to a bench and pulled her down next to him. "I don't want to fight with you, Abby." He took her hands in his.

She looked into his sincere gaze and felt lost. "I don't want to fight either. But I can't stop thinking about her." She glanced down at their hands. "Every time you touch me, I feel guilty." The words were barely a whisper.

"Don't." He put a finger under her chin to lift her face. "We're not doing anything wrong."

"Aren't we?"

"No. We're both caught up in something beyond our control. We're making the best of a difficult situation. There's nothing wrong with having a little fun while we're at it."

What kind of fun was Noah referring to? The kind he usually had while on a trip? Fun like they'd had back in their hotel on Key West? Abby couldn't shake the memory. Did Noah think about it too?

Or was it just one of many similar encounters he'd had over the years? With nameless, faceless women.

She shrugged off the disturbing thought.

They wouldn't be having any more of that kind of fun.

Noah squeezed her hand. "So, are we okay?"

"Yeah, we're okay."

He exhaled. "Good." He kissed her forehead. "Why don't you buy Claire something?"

"Buy her something? Like a souvenir?"

"Sure. Why not?"

"I don't think she'll want a souvenir from our honeymoon."

"See, you need to stop thinking of it like that. Don't think of it as a honeymoon. Think of it as a great vacation."

"I really don't think—"

"I do." Noah rose and tugged her from the bench. "She'll know you were thinking about her. A lot." A slight trace of disapproval still tinged his voice.

Abby followed him, not sure buying Claire something was the best course of action. The way Claire'd been acting lately, she'd be sure to take it the wrong way.

"What would she like?"

"I don't know." She couldn't muster much enthusiasm for the idea.

"Come on, Abby."

"Fine." She thought for a moment. "Jewelry. Claire loves jewelry."

"Terrific. We passed a jewelry store as we were walking. We'll check it out on the way back to the ship."

Together they decided on a pair of earrings, but Abby insisted on paying for them herself. A joint gift would not be the way to go.

Chapter Ten

Dinner that night was another extravagant affair, but Abby declined Noah's offer to stroll around the decks afterward, claiming a touch of seasickness. The ship needed to make large circles in the Gulf of Mexico to avoid getting into their next port too early, and she did look a bit pasty.

He reclined on the bed, waiting for her to emerge from the bathroom. She'd been quiet at dinner, but he had the feeling seasickness wasn't to blame. Something had changed between them, and he wasn't sure what or how it had happened. But the easygoing mood of Key West had vanished. Before, she'd been nervous around him sometimes, but now she wasn't nervous. She wasn't anything.

She'd shut him out.

Despite the enjoyable day they'd had, something was wrong. Ever since they'd talked about Claire, Abby had acted differently.

It upset him to think she was feeling so guilty about Claire. But he didn't know how to fix it.

His earlier words were true. They were in a situation beyond their control. That Claire had gotten them into. If anyone should be feeling guilty, it should be Claire. For putting Abby through this.

He didn't buy it that Claire had done it for him. Or that she had any kind of strong feelings for him. He'd known a lot of women like Claire. Their feelings were superficial at best.

But what had she hoped to gain from the whole game show thing? Why have Abby take her place? Wouldn't it have been better to have just canceled?

It sure would have saved everyone, herself included, a lot of needless aggravation and anxiety.

Before he could think about it further, the bathroom door opened. Abby stood in the doorway, looking even paler than before. One hand clutched the frame, her knuckles white.

"Are you okay?"

Abby nodded, but then shook her head. "No. I really don't feel so well."

"Come here, you need to lie down." He got up and took her hand, leading her to the bed. "There, scoot under the covers." He drew the sheet over her legs as she lay back on the pillow and closed her eyes. He put his hand on her forehead, relieved that it felt cool to his touch.

"Let's get some fresh air in here." He propped open the balcony door with one of their suitcases. "There. That's better."

He sat down on the side of the bed. She opened her eyes and gave him a weak smile.

"Is there anything I can do?" He'd been seasick on a sailboat outing across Lake Michigan and sympathized with the awful feeling.

"Not unless you can make the boat stop turning."

"Unfortunately, that I can't do. How about some ginger ale? That might help settle your stomach."

"Mmmm, hmmmm," Abby mumbled.

"Okay, I'll run downstairs and get you something." He started for the door but then turned. "Are you going to be all right while I'm gone."

"Fine." Her eyes closed again.

"I'll be quick." He didn't wait for an answer before heading out the door.

By the time he returned with Abby's ginger ale she had fallen asleep. A good night's sleep would have her feeling better in the morning. When she woke, they'd be anchored off of Calica, Mexico, and the circling would have stopped. He set the drink on the nightstand and contemplated what to do.

With the balcony door open, there wasn't enough room for him to sleep on the floor on that side of the bed. The fresh air was better for Abby than the stuffy cool of the air-conditioning, so he didn't want to close the door. If he slept on the bathroom side, she might trip over him if she got up in the middle of the night. And there wasn't enough space between the foot of the bed and the cabin wall.

For half a second he entertained the thought of crawling into bed with her, but after the strange way she'd acted all day, he figured she'd be upset to find him there if she woke up before he did in the morning.

After one final glimpse at Abby's peaceful, sleeping face, he turned off the light, then walked out on the balcony. He sat down in one of the chairs and pulled the other over to prop his feet on.

Not the best, but it would do. He closed his eyes.

****

The next morning Abby declared she felt much better, but she wasn't quite herself on the tender ride to shore. Whether she still felt sick or something else troubled her, Noah couldn't begin to guess.

He shifted on the bench. His muscles ached from sleeping upright all night in the chairs. He rubbed the back of his neck.

"What's wrong?"

He stopped. "Nothing."

"Noah."

At that he laughed. "This conversation is sounding familiar. But isn't it usually the other way around? Most of the time I need to convince you to tell me what's wrong."

Abby laughed, and he was heartened to hear the sound was genuine.

"Really, what's wrong with your neck?"

"It's a little stiff. Slept funny last night."

Abby leaned in closer, then looked around as if to make sure no one could overhear them. "Well, those chairs couldn't have been comfortable. Why didn't you sleep on the floor again?"

He shrugged. "I wanted to keep the balcony door open so you'd have some fresh air. There wasn't room on the floor."

"Oh." Abby didn't seem to know what to say to that.

He reached over and patted her hand. "Don't worry, it'll be fine. Nothing an hour-long bus ride won't cure." Once ashore they'd transfer to a bus that would take them to the famous Mayan ruins at Tulum.

Abby opened her mouth, but shut it again when he leaned closer to whisper in her ear. "Now, start pretending that you still like me, I'm sure there are cameras around here some place." He kissed her cheek, inhaling the sweet lilac scent of her hair before moving away, but didn't let go of her hand.

He'd said the words in jest, but there was an underlying truth to them. Did Abby like him anymore? Hell, maybe she'd never liked him.

He toyed with the bracelet on her wrist, running his fingers over the silver chain, then the smooth skin beneath. Her hand twitched.

Unbidden, the feel of her in his arms back in Key West jumped into his mind. The memory of her passionate response to his kiss had him shifting in his seat.

The kiss had been instinctive. He hadn't thought about it. Covering her mouth with his own and bringing her body close to his had seemed like the right thing to do.

All rational thought had fled when she'd wrapped her arms around him and kissed him back.

But just because she'd responded so

passionately to his kisses didn't mean anything. Maybe she was really good at pretending.

Almost as quickly as the thought formed, he pushed it away. Everything about Abby was genuine. She had to have honestly felt something back at the hotel. So what was the problem now?

To distract himself, he asked her to read aloud from the tour literature she had grabbed before leaving the ship.

She obliged, reciting from the brochure in a Julie McCoy voice. "Tulum dates back from the time of the waning of the Mayan civilization. The structures found there are comparatively small, especially El Castillo, the area's most prominent structure. Tulum is the only Mayan city known to have been encircled by a wall fortification, and it's the only Mayan city known to be a coastal community." She paused and looked over at him. "Sounds pretty cool."

After a brief stop at a small roadside market, they arrived at their destination. Noah stared up at the great, crumbling structures, feeling small and insignificant next to the towering ruins. He tried to visualize how they might have looked in the past, untouched by the ravages of time.

His hands itched for his own camera, but before he could indulge, he and Abby were obligated to pose for pictures and stroll through the ruins for the video cameras.

After what seemed like hours, they were granted time to explore on their own. Noah, much more at home behind the lens of a camera than in front of it, took pictures of the awe-inspiring sight before him. Out of the corner of his eye, he saw Abby wander around the side of one of the crumbling structures.

As he tried to focus on the outline of the ancient ruins against the azure sky, his thoughts weren't ever far from her. The memory of the curve of her cheek as it rested against her pillow the night before seemed to be burned into his brain like an image on a negative. He couldn't get it out of his mind. He was drawn to her in a way he had never experienced before, and he didn't know what to make of it.

He'd snapped the last picture on the roll of film when her cry of pain reached his ears. By the time he rounded the corner of the building where she'd disappeared, a small crowd had gathered around her. She sat on one of the jagged rocks, clutching her ankle.

"Excuse me, let me through, please. That's my wife." He didn't question the words that sprang to his lips, or the concern-roughened edge to his voice.

The crowd parted to let him through. He went down on one knee beside her. "Abby, honey, what happened?"

Through a haze of tears, she looked up at him. His heart tightened at the pain reflected in her eyes.

"A misstep, that's all."

"Your ankle?"

She nodded as he pushed her hands away to examine the injury.

"I'm sorry," he said when she winced. "That hurts?" He moved her foot as gently as he could.

She sucked in a breath, then nodded again.

"We need to get ice on this."

"There's some in a cooler on the bus. I'll go get it." One of the men in the crowd turned and headed toward the parking area.

"I have a better idea." Noah scooped Abby into his arms and stood. "Let's get you to the bus so we can get that boot off. Hang on."

Abby looped her arms around his neck and nestled her head into his shoulder. The trust in that simple gesture tugged at his soul. His long strides ate up the distance to the bus in a matter of minutes. Soon he had her settled, her ice-wrapped foot propped up on the seat across the aisle.

"Feeling better?" He tucked a loose strand of hair back behind her ear.

"Yes." She touched his face. "Thank you."

His gaze locked with hers. After the aloofness of yesterday and this morning, it seemed an oddly intimate gesture.

"You always take such good care of me." Tears shimmered in her eyes once again.

"Abby?"

"You're a good man, Noah Grant." She leaned forward and pressed a kiss to his mouth.

His first instinct was to deepen the kiss. But he resisted the urge. Letting Abby take control was infinitely more pleasing. She'd never initiated kissing him before.

Had he ever been kissed like this before? Abby's kiss was sweet and gentle and...sincere. No hidden agendas. No means to an end. No thoughts of what it would lead to.

And although he instinctively knew the kiss wasn't meant to arouse, his body responded immediately. His heart knocked against his ribs. Heat flooded through him. He hardened.

Her tongue touched his.

A bolt of white-hot lightning shot through him.

Unable to hold back any longer, he gathered her into his arms and deepened the kiss. His vows to not kiss her again fled as she whimpered beneath the probing caress of his mouth. He drank in the sweet taste of her. His fingers speared into her hair, holding her against his seeking mouth.

The kiss changed.

From sweet to sensual. From gentle to passionate. From innocent to carnal. Abby responded to his insistence and kissed him back with a desire that equaled his own.

Through the sexual haze clouding his mind, he became aware of the other members of the tour group boarding the bus, and he withdrew.

Her chest rose and fell with her harsh breathing, and he struggled to draw air into his lungs as well. Their eyes met and held for long seconds, before the chattering crowd broke the spell.

He settled himself in the seat next to her, willing his racing pulse to return to normal, then tenderly shifted her injured foot into his lap. Although he'd like nothing better than to keep kissing Abby, he contented himself with cradling her legs across his knees for the return trip to the tender.

****

With Noah's help Abby hobbled from the bus to the tender and then to their cabin. She sank onto the bed. He arranged a stack of pillows underneath her foot.

"Do you want me to get the ship's doctor?" His voice still held the note of concern it had taken on as he'd pushed his way through the crowd to get to her earlier.

"No, don't be silly. It's only a sprain. I'll be up and about in no time at all." She refused to dwell on the irony of Claire's sprained ankle being the reason Abby was here with Noah in the first place.

"Are you sure?"

A knock on the door interrupted their conversation. Noah opened the door to a cabin steward, who entered and placed an ice bucket on the nightstand.

"How are you feeling, Mrs. Grant?"

She started at the words, then darted a look at Noah. No one had referred to her that way before.

"Much better, thank you. And thank you for the ice."

"Is there anything else I can get you?"

"No, this will be fine."

"I thought you might want something to look at." He handed her a stack of magazines.

"Thank you," she said again.

Noah, who hovered in the background, stepped forward. "Is it possible to get dinner delivered to our cabin tonight? I don't think my wife is up to going to the dining room."

Her pulse skittered. Had he referred to her as his wife in front of the steward on purpose, or had the words slipped out as they seemed to earlier at the ruins?

"No problem, Mr. Grant. I'll make arrangements with the dining room and bring it up for you."

"Thank you." Noah ushered the man out the door. "We'd really appreciate that."

Once the man had gone, Noah returned and examined her ankle, running his hands over the slight swelling.

She sucked in her breath. A shiver of awareness shot through her. Heat spread through her limbs.

"Still hurts? Let's keep ice on it." Noah stood and disappeared into the bathroom.

She let out her breath. His touch hadn't hurt at all. Not unless sensual pleasure counted as pain. Had her ankle always been an erogenous point, or was it Noah that inflamed her?

He returned with a washcloth, which he filled with ice then placed on her foot. "Better?"

She nodded. She'd like to pack her whole body in ice. How could such a simple, innocent touch affect her so much?

"Want to watch some TV while we wait for dinner?"

"Sounds good to me."

Noah joined her on the bed and grabbed the remote. But as he surfed through the channels, her mind drifted from the images flickering across the screen.

The man beside her remained a mystery. Yesterday she had resolved not to let him get to her anymore, not to be affected by his natural charm. But he had been so caring last night when she wasn't feeling well. And today at the ruins. She'd never forget the look on his face as he'd made his way toward her. Or the tone of his voice when he'd called her his wife.

Then she'd kissed him. She hadn't been able to help herself.

And he'd kissed her. Her token of affection and gratitude had turned into something much, much more. Her stomach quivered at the memory. And she'd melted when he had innocently touched her ankle. So much for resolve.

Problem was, she liked Noah. She couldn't deny it. No matter how she felt about his attitude toward commitment and relationships, she liked him. And she liked the person she was when she was with him. She was adventurous and spontaneous and unlike herself. Wouldn't you know it? She liked being fun.

So that was that. She'd go with the flow. At least until the end of their cruise. Then she could go back to being her usual, predictable, ordinary self. But for now she'd enjoy every moment she could. Most of all the moments with Noah.

Even the ones that made her body hum and her pulse race.

To distract herself from the heat still flowing through her veins, she picked up one of the magazines the steward had left. She flipped through it until a series of vivid pictures caught her eye. One showed a cliff, the jagged rocks jutting toward a turquoise sky. Below, waves crashed against the base, raising a spray of froth and foam. Another showed the face of the cliff, the sky a canopy overhead, as if the photographer were suspended from the rock itself. The third, taken from on top of the cliff, was of the sun dipping into the water, setting it afire with its glow. The wild beauty of the images stole her breath.

"Wow."

Noah glanced over at her and raised an eyebrow.

"Look at these pictures. Aren't they amazing? I can almost hear the waves crashing against the rocks."

He peered at the pictures, but looked back to the TV almost immediately. "Uh, yeah, they're great."

"What?" she teased. "Can't you look at photographs that aren't yours?"

Noah looked over. "Don't be silly."

"Then look at this. I can't get over how beautiful this is. I wonder where they were taken."

"South America."

She glanced at him. "How do you know that?"

He didn't look at her. "Because I took them."

"Oh." She studied the pictures once again. The scene was primitive, dangerous. A place untouched by most human eyes.

It told her a lot about the man sitting beside her, providing a mirror into his soul.

No one could hold a man who took such wild, untamed photographs.

Chapter Eleven

The next day they were at sea and were able to spend time alone without the hindering presence of the TV show's cameras and video crew. Lazing around by the pool took up much of the day, and Abby returned to the cabin with Noah in the late afternoon feeling sun-kissed and content. Even the soreness in her ankle had subsided.

She collapsed on the bed and sighed, closing her eyes. "Now that's what I call getting away from it all."

The mattress dipped, and she opened one lazy eye. Noah reclined on his back beside her. His tan had deepened, and he looked sexy and bronzed wearing only his swim trunks. She quelled the urge to turn toward him.

"There's a party on deck tonight."

She shook her head. "I don't want to move."

Noah rolled onto his side to face her, propping himself up on one elbow. "Don't be a spoilsport. It'll be fun."

She stuck her tongue out at him.

He laughed as he rose from the bed, grabbed her arm, and pulled her up too. "C'mon, I'll even let you shower first."

A festive mood greeted them when they walked onto the deck later that night. Colorful lanterns dotted the air. A steel-drum band played rhythmic music as dancers gathered around the pool.

"Wow, some party," Abby said.

"I'll say." Noah took her hand as a group of passengers jostled by. "How's the ankle feeling?"

She tested by shifting her weight. Sore, but not too bad. "It'll hold up as long as I don't do any of that dancing." She nodded toward the pool deck, which pulsed with a life of its own. Hundreds of people crowded on it.

"Okay, so no dancing. How about something to eat?" Noah nodded at a waiter passing by with a tray laden with tropical fruit.

She laughed. "I bet I've gained fifty pounds on this cruise already."

Noah's eyes swept down her body.

"I don't think you need to worry about that." He used his index finger to trace the small strip of bare skin visible on her stomach where her shirt didn't quite meet the waist of her skirt.

She sucked in her breath.

His eyes sought hers. "Ticklish?"

"Yes," she lied.

Noah's lips quirked, but didn't quite form into a full smile. "Interesting." He gazed at her a moment longer before breaking eye contact. "C'mon, let's get a drink."

She followed as he tugged on her hand. A good stiff drink sounded like just the thing. Or a dip in the pool, providing the water was ice cold. Noah's touch on her flesh hadn't tickled at all. It had, however, sent heat radiating over her skin.

"Rum punch?" He asked as they reached a bar on the far side of the deck.

"Sure."

As the festivities went on around them, she and Noah consumed decadent treats from the food stations set up along the outer edges of the deck. Sometimes they chatted, other times they fell silent.

Women who passed by the table cast covetous glances at Noah, but to Abby's secret delight, he paid them no heed. He seemed oblivious to the parade of bikini-clad females who sauntered by, swinging their hips suggestively.

For her part, she found it difficult to keep her eyes off him. He'd left the top few buttons of his flamboyant Hawaiian shirt open, affording her tantalizing glimpses of his bare chest every time he moved. He'd been shirtless all afternoon, but somehow, this was sexier.

A warm, salty breeze blew across the Gulf. She rolled the frosty drink glass across her forehead, blaming the humid air for her rising temperature.

Noah's eyes tracked the movement of her glass, then caught and held hers. "C'mon." He rose from his chair and offered his hand. "We can dance to this."

The band had switched to a slower rhythm, and couples swayed on the makeshift dance floor.

"I don't think—"

"C'mon." Noah tugged her from her chair. He led her to the floor, then turned, and pulled her into his arms. One strong hand splayed across her back, the other cradled her palm in his. She rested her free hand on his shoulder as they shuffled their feet to the slow beat of the music. Only a few inches separated their bodies. Heat radiated from him. Heat that had nothing to do with the sultry night air.

As more couples joined those already on the deck, it became difficult to move. As they were jostled once again, Noah pulled her tighter against him. The heat flowed from his body into hers. Like a fever, the warmth raced through her, setting her afire. A slow ache spread.

Noah's hand drifted to the small of her back. His fingers stroked the strip of bare skin there. She shifted closer to the hard contours of his body. Her arm curved around his back. Her head nestled into his shoulder, and she breathed in the crisp scent of his aftershave. She could spend the next million years listening to the steady strum of his pulse.

"Soft," he whispered. "Your skin is so soft."

She lifted her head to gaze up at him.

"Oh, Abby, what are you doing to me?" He lowered his lips to hers. His kiss was warm and soft. She melted at the sweet pressure. Never mind what she did to him, what about what he did to her?

Noah kept the kiss short. He pulled his mouth from hers to string soft kisses along her jaw, until he touched the tender spot behind her ear with the tip of his tongue.

She bit her lip to keep from moaning. Delicate shivers danced along the nerve endings of her body.

"Let's get out of here."

Noah's husky voice in her ear turned the shivers to a shudder. The ache intensified.

She nodded, not trusting herself to speak. He led her off the crowded dance floor and away from the crush of people. He rounded a corner and then pulled her into his arms. The noise of the party faded as his mouth claimed hers. Gone was the gentle, tender caress from a few moments earlier. This kiss was deep, hard, and possessive.

Abby couldn't help the involuntary whimper that escaped when his tongue delved into the recesses of her mouth. Although she didn't think it possible, Noah brought her even closer, melding their bodies into one. His hands cupped her hips, lifting and pressing her into the cradle of his thighs. She pulled her mouth from his and gasped at the thrust of his arousal.

He shifted, raising her leg so she rode his thigh. He flexed, rubbing her.

"Noah." His name escaped on a shuddering sigh.

He looked deep into her eyes, his own heavy with desire. "I want to make love to you, Abby."

She was too far gone to think about why it wasn't a good idea. She wouldn't think about what would happen tomorrow or the next day. She couldn't deny what she wanted anymore. She wanted Noah. To be wrapped in his arms and have him fulfill the promise she read in his passion-darkened eyes.

So she raised her face to his. "Yes." She pressed her mouth to his.

He groaned, kissing her with fierce need before pulling away. "Let's go."

His voice sounded rough, and a fine tremor shook the hand that held hers. It took him two tries to get their cabin door open, but once inside, silence descended. They stood and stared at one another. After what seemed like an eternity, Noah stepped toward her and raised a hand to frame the side of her face. His thumb stroked over her cheek.

"Are you sure?"

The care and concern reflected in his eyes touched her. He would shelve his own desire if she was unsure. It made her want him more. And she was tired of pretending she didn't, so she nodded, a small smile on her lips. "I'm sure."

Noah closed his eyes for a brief moment. When he opened them, the look in the blue orbs took her breath away. It brought to mind visions of growing old and happily ever after. But she refused to dwell on that. She focused instead on the delicious shiver that consumed her when he wrapped his arms around her and drew her into his embrace.

His gentle, coaxing mouth covered hers, as if seeking further assurance she wanted him. His fingers found the strip of bare skin at her middle. He stroked the flesh there, then moved his hands higher, pushing the fabric of her shirt up as he went. She raised her arms as he drew it over her head, then lowered her hands to the buttons of his shirt as hers fell to the ground.

Her fingers trembled as she unfastened the

buttons, then pushed the fabric apart. She flattened her hands against him. His muscles bunched and flexed as he shrugged out of the shirt, allowing it to fall in a careless heap on the floor. Beneath her palm the heavy thud of his heartbeat accelerated when she leaned into him and pressed an open-mouthed kiss to the pulse at the base of his neck. His skin was smooth and hot beneath her hands. She reveled in the pleasure of being able to touch him so intimately.

"Oh, God, Abby. I can't believe—" He stopped when her hands drifted to the waistband of his shorts and unfastened them. He swallowed, and tried again. "I've been dreaming about touching you like this all week. I never thought—"

She cut him off. "Don't," she whispered. "Don't think." She wanted him to be as mindless as she was.

His hands undid the knot of fabric at her waist. Her skirt fell to join the pile of clothing on the floor at their feet.

His trembling fingers found the front clasp of her bra, and it too fell away, leaving her bare to his gaze.

And his touch. She shivered as he stroked her skin, starting on her stomach and working his way higher until he cupped her breast. He traced the pad of his thumb over the nipple, barely grazing it. It tightened into a firm bud, and her head fell back. She gasped. Noah ran a trail of kisses along the exposed column of her throat. When he reached her collarbone, he nipped it with his teeth. She shuddered. Her knees went weak, and she fell against him.

He scooped her into his arms. In one stride he crossed to the bed. He gazed at her, desire etched into the lines of his face. She raised her arms to him, and he joined her, coming down next to her and rolling her to her side so she faced him. He brushed the hair from her face, then cupped her cheek and brought her mouth to his for a soul-deep kiss that curled her toes.

Without breaking the kiss, he shifted her onto her back, following and fitting his body over hers. The erotic weight of his chest crushed her. He left her mouth to string a line of kisses down her throat. When he reached the curve of her breast, he sucked on the rounded flesh. His mouth closed over her nipple and pulled it into the heat of his mouth. His tongue flicked over the very tip. She arched her back and bunched handfuls of the bedspread into her fists.

Her head tossed on the pillow as he continued his sensual assault, and her nails bit into his shoulder. They dug deeper when he moved to the other breast and lavished the same attention on it.

Echoes of their harsh breathing reverberated through the small cabin.

"Noah," she gasped. She was ready. She wanted him. Now.

He seemed to read the desperation in her eyes and voice. "Almost, sweetheart. Almost."

His tongue circled, then dipped into her navel. She squirmed. If he went any further she'd come apart. In desperation she wove her fingers through his hair and tugged.

"Please. We've waited long enough."

For a moment, she didn't think he'd heed her plea as his hand drifted beneath the waistband of her panties. He pulled the lacy garment down her legs and off, tossing it to the side before sliding out of his boxers.

He kissed his way back up her body, starting with her ankles, sliding warm, wet kisses across her calves and over her knees. His breath stirred the curls at the juncture of her thighs as his lips whispered past, but he didn't stop until he'd reached her mouth. By then fine tremors shook her entire body.

His kiss was hungry, passionate, as he stretched his body over hers. She tore her mouth from his with a gasp as their naked bodies touched from chest to thigh. He pressed, bare and full and hard, against her. A jolt shot through her core. She needed to touch him. Her hands slid down his body, but before she'd reached her goal, Noah captured them in his.

She raised questioning eyes to his. "I want to touch you."

He groaned, the sound raw and grating in his throat, then kissed her once again. "I know." His voice shook around the words. "But if you touch me now..." He let his voice trail off.

"Later," he promised. He brought her hand to his mouth and kissed the delicate silver chain that lay across the fluttering pulse at her wrist.

Abby squirmed beneath him. If he wasn't going to let her touch him, then she wanted him inside her.

"One more minute." He tore open a condom packet.

A whimper escaped from her throat when he pulled away. She tugged him back to her. She couldn't wait any longer.

He levered himself up on his arms, poised over her. He slid into her. Inch by delicious inch he pushed deeper, until at last he'd sheathed his entire fullness within her.

He held still and looked into her eyes. He kissed her. Then he moved. He pulled back, then slid forward, each time touching her more deeply.

She wrapped her arms around his shoulders and pulled him down toward her, welcoming his weight once again. Her hips rose to meet his. Matched his rhythm. She wanted it to last forever. This moment.

Here in Noah's arms. Him buried inside her.

But it couldn't last, because already her lower body trembled, and as he slid into her again, she tightened herself around him. Fingers of heat radiated from her core and raced along her nerve endings. The wave of pleasure seemed to last for an eternity, but even as she came down, Noah shuddered over her, and for a brief moment he collapsed on her, his breath harsh in her ear.

She held him to her, not willing to let him go. Not wanting reality to intrude into the paradise she'd found in his arms. But as the tremors in both their bodies faded away, he eased back. He kissed her, then looked into her eyes.

What did he see there? Too exhausted to shutter her emotions, she had the feeling he could see into her soul, where a piece of him now resided.

He opened his mouth, as if to say something. She raised her lips to his and silenced him with a kiss. She didn't want any words. Words would ruin it.

He seemed to understand. Kissing her one more time, he rolled away for a brief moment, then returned and enclosed her in his embrace, so she lay cradled against him in the curve of his arm. As they drifted off into sleep, the soft touch of his lips brushed her hair, and she knew without a doubt, as if there had been any before, that she was in deep. She had done the most foolish thing she could have done.

She'd fallen in love with her husband.

Chapter Twelve

She was in love with Noah.

Although she woke with the first rays of the sun coming through the blinds, Abby lay still, feeling the steady rise and fall of his chest where it pressed against her back. His breath whispered in her ear.

Was it even possible to love someone she'd known for such a short time? As she lay curled against him, his arm warm and heavy around her waist, the answer came. Without a doubt she could.

She stretched her legs. A slight twinge of soreness in her lower body evoked erotic memories. Twice during the night Noah had awakened her with sensual kisses that had soon left her aching and trembling for more. She'd found unparalleled pleasure in his arms.

He stirred behind her, then his soft whisper reached her. "Morning."

She turned toward him and echoed his greeting, offering a shy smile. The cover of darkness had made it easy to abandon her self-consciousness, but in the light of day, she was all too aware of the wanton and intimate acts they'd indulged in during the night. She now knew every wonderful inch of Noah's body, and he hers.

But his smile was tender as he raised a hand to brush a strand of hair out of her eyes. He tucked the wisp behind her ear, then lingered to trace the shell with his fingertips.

She shivered. Who would have thought that so many parts of her body could be erogenous zones? Noah had found each and every one of them during the course of the night.

Although the pleasure of his touch on her ear was compelling, she had more immediate needs. She pushed him away when he leaned toward her.

"I need to get up."

"I'm already up."

At that she laughed, but rolled away from him anyway. Sliding from beneath the covers, she pulled the sheet with her, wrapping it around her body as she rose from the bed.

Unconcerned with his nudity, Noah relaxed against the pillows, grinning when her gaze drifted lower, then widened at the proof of his words. He hadn't been kidding.

"Don't be long." A wicked gleam lit his eye.

Still laughing, Abby hurried into the bathroom.

She took care of what she needed to and had finished brushing her teeth when the door opened. Noah walked in. Still resplendently naked and aroused, he reached around her for his own toothbrush, meeting her gaze in the mirror.

Sharing a bathroom, especially one this tiny, wasn't something she was used to, but Abby liked the forced intimacy. Noah finished with his toothbrush and replaced it next to the sink. Then he reached for her.

His good morning kiss sent small ripples of shock waves through her. She tasted the minty flavor of his toothpaste as their breath mingled.

He pulled away, a thoughtful look on his face. "Do you think that shower will hold both of us?"

"Are you kidding? That shower barely holds me," she protested.

Noah reached past her to turn on the water. "I bet we can make it work." He unwound the sheet from her body and nudged her into the stall.

****

The schedule for the day had them booked on a

sightseeing tour in Grand Cayman, which included a long stop at the famous Seven Mile Beach. They took a tender to shore, taking some time to wander through the shopping district before their tour departed. The film crew from the TV show took only a few minutes of video before letting them know they'd meet them on the bus.

Abby strolled hand in hand with Noah through the small shops, not lingering too long in any particular one, but enjoying the atmosphere of the tropical island setting. She tried to convince herself that nothing had changed, but recognized the thought for the lie it was.

Everything had changed. She now knew the man walking beside her as intimately as she knew herself. She knew every inch of his body, down to the tiny scar low on his back above his left hip. In the shower that morning she'd noticed the scratches on his back where her nails had raked his flesh. Her breast wore the faint trace of the love bite he had bestowed there.

Physical marks of possession weren't the ones she worried about. In time those would fade, but the mark he'd left on her soul wouldn't be as easy to heal. How could she have been so foolish as to fall in love with a man who had no desire to be loved?

She and Noah still played a game. That part hadn't changed. But when he stopped and plucked a brilliant orange and gold hibiscus blossom from a tree along their path and tucked it behind her ear, she lost a little bit more of her heart to him in the romantic sweetness of the simple gesture.

From time to time Noah stopped to snap pictures. His face wore an expression of supreme satisfaction while doing so.

"Have you always wanted to be a photographer?" she asked.

"Pretty much. My mom's an artist, so I think I

get it from her."

"Really? Does she paint for a living?"

Noah's face clouded. "No, she just dabbles now. She's really talented. Works mostly in watercolors. She had a promising career ahead of her before she met my dad."

Abby heard the unspoken word in Noah's sentence. "But?"

His gaze met hers for a brief moment, before he looked away. "But she had to give it all up when she had me."

She hated the flat tone of his voice. Why did he harbor so much guilt about his parents and the life they led? After a moment of uncomfortable silence, the first of the day, she felt brave enough to ask, "You blame yourself because she gave it up?"

Noah stopped walking, dropped her hand, and ran his fingers through his hair. "Yes."

"But why?" She needed to let it go, but couldn't. "Did she tell you that?"

"Heck no. She's happy with her life." He paused. "But she could have had so much more." He spoke the last words almost to himself. He resumed walking.

She followed, pondering his words. To her, they still didn't make sense. "Did she ever say she wanted more?"

Noah looked over at her, then shook his head. "No."

"But obviously you know the story of your conception."

"Of course. It's the big family joke. 'Dad couldn't keep his hands off Mom.' He still can't."

Abby's mouth dropped open. "Your parents talk about sex in front of you?"

"All the time. What, yours don't?"

"Never. In fact, I'm convinced my parents never had sex at all. I'm sure I'm the result of some top secret military biological experiment."

Noah laughed. "Nice."

They walked on for a while, until she picked up the earlier thread of their conversation. "When did you start taking pictures?"

"I got my first camera for my birthday when I turned ten. One of those cheap, disposable ones, but I couldn't get enough of it. I loved taking pictures of anything and everything. My brothers and sisters got a kick out of doing crazy things for me, so I could get it all on film. It thrilled me to get those pictures back and see those images captured for all time. Mom's got a billion photo albums. It became such a passion, I knew it was what I wanted to do when I grew up."

"When do you think that will be?" she teased.

"Never, I hope," he bantered back.

"Is that what you studied in college?"

"Yep. And that's when I started to travel. I did a couple of internships for travel magazines while working on my degree, and I realized what I'd been missing out on all those years. There was a whole world outside of small-town Indiana waiting for me to explore. My parents wouldn't get to see it, but I made a vow then and there, I wouldn't miss any of it. And with my photographs I'm able to bring a little of it back with me for them."

Abby sighed. With Noah it always came back to the same thing. His parents missing out because of him. He had built his whole world around, what seemed to her, misplaced guilt. It had formed who he was and how he viewed the world. He carried the burden of it around, and she couldn't change that. She couldn't strip away a lifetime of guilt in one short week, even if it had been her place to try.

Even if he was the man she loved.

But she couldn't stop herself from making one more comment. "I'm sure your parents love the pictures you bring back, but I bet they'd love it even more if you weren't gone so often. From what you've said, it seems to me like their family means the world to them." Was his family aware of the guilt that gnawed at him?

Noah fell silent.

She bit her lip. Had she offended him?

The silence stretched until Abby could no longer stand the tension she'd created between them. She placed a hand on his arm. He glanced down at her.

"I'm sorry. It wasn't my place to say that."

For a moment she wasn't sure if Noah would acknowledge her apology, but then he surprised her by pulling her into his arms right there in the middle of the sidewalk. His move was so sudden that several tourists behind them had to make a quick change in direction to avoid running into them.

Ignoring the disgruntled expressions of the people around them, Abby rested her head against Noah's shoulder and wrapped her arms around his waist, loving the feel of his arms around her. She inhaled. The sexy scent of his aftershave brought back vivid memories of his skin against hers.

"You don't need to be sorry." He kissed the top of her head. He released her but kept one arm around her shoulders. They continued their leisurely stroll.

"So, your parents would never have walked down the street like this?" Noah asked after a moment.

"Nope. There were always appearances to keep up."

"What about you?"

"What do you mean, what about me?"

"How do you feel about public displays of affection?"

"Are you kidding? With all of the cameras and video people following us around all week, not to mention the rest of the people staring at us, there hasn't been much that hasn't been public affection, now has there?"

Noah guided her into a small alley between two stores, out of the flow of pedestrian traffic on the sidewalk. His hands wrapped around her upper arms, and of their own volition, hers raised to flatten against his chest. The steady thud of his heart beat against her palm. The noise of the nearby street faded away.

"There was last night." The words, low and intimate, fell over her like a lover's caress. The kiss that followed spoke of all the secret intimacies they had shared.

Several long, sensual minutes later, he broke the kiss to rest his forehead against hers. The erratic pace of his breathing matched her own. The pulse of his heartbeat beneath her hands came quicker now. On a deep inhale of air, he opened his eyes. "If we didn't have to catch that damn bus in ten minutes—" He left the provocative threat unfinished.

The depth of her disappointment shocked Abby. Holding hands in public was one thing, but making love? Although she was not as prudish as her parents, before this week the mere suggestion would have been enough to bring a blush to her cheeks. Now she trembled with an unfulfilled need that she would have gladly assuaged then and there. What was happening to her?

Noah smiled. "I guess we'll have to wait until later."

On the bus Abby had a hard time focusing on anything the guide said, even though the tour was supposed to be one of the best on the island. The first stop was Hell.

Aptly named.

Noah had ignited a fire within her, and only he could put it out. How would she make it through the next three and a half hours in her own personal hell before they'd be alone again?

Hell, the tourist spot, was an area of land named by a man, who upon seeing the strange rock formation there, had thought it must be what hell looked like.

Noah addressed several postcards to friends of his and sent them from the post office, where they were stamped "from Hell". Abby declined doing the same, reminding him she had no desire to let anyone know where she was. "This fun adventure is our little secret, remember?"

"How could I forget?"

From there they headed to the Turtle Farm. The reptilian creatures fascinated her. They ranged in size from a few ounces to giant ones weighing more than five hundred pounds. It saddened her that the ancient creatures were near extinction, and she hoped the Farm's efforts to preserve them would be successful.

The film crew followed their every move, but she'd grown used to them. Their presence no longer bothered her. Most of the time she barely noticed they were there.

Finally they arrived at Seven Mile Beach, the highlight of the tour. She and Noah posed for cheesy pictures while they sipped frosty glasses of a tropical beverage with their arms entwined.

Noah grimaced as a drop of the red liquid dripped down his chin and onto his shirt. He looked at the mark with disgust. "Really?" he muttered. "Who actually does this? You can't drink like this."

She laughed, wiping ineffectually at the spot with her fingers once they'd untangled their arms.

On impulse, she fisted his collar in her hand and brought his face down for a kiss. "Mmmm," she said in appreciation. "You taste like kiwi." She ran her tongue over his lower lip.

His head jerked back. He gazed down at her, his

eyes smoldering. She wanted to lose herself in the heat and passion of his gaze.

She leaned toward him, but then at the last second remembered they weren't alone. With a quick glance at the television people surrounding them, she offered Noah a regretful smile.

"Soon," he whispered, his voice a husky promise in her ear.

After they finished with the cameras and crew, they were directed to the changing rooms, where they donned the swim gear they'd brought with them. They locked their belongings in the private cabana provided for them, then headed out to enjoy the expansive stretch of white sandy beach.

****

After taking a quick dip in the turquoise blue water, Noah nodded toward the lounging chairs dotting the beach. "Sit or walk?"

Abby eyed the hordes of sun-worshippers gathered there. "Walk."

"Sounds good to me." He took her hand, and they strolled down the beach, away from the throng of people. Not bothering with a towel, he let the heat from the sun's rays dry the water from his chest and shoulders.

In deference to the hot sand, they walked in the surf surging onto the shore. The waves sucked at their feet before returning to the sea in an endless cycle. Abby remained silent, which left him to dwell on their earlier conversation.

His parents had never told him they felt cheated by the hand life had dealt them, but to him they had been. How could they be content with a life in the middle of nowhere Indiana when there was a whole world out there they'd never see? They had to feel like they were missing out, didn't they?

He'd never questioned his feelings before. Had always assumed, by sharing his photographs with them, he was allowing them to experience a part of life they'd been denied.

For as long as he could remember, he'd made it his goal to not only see as much of the world as he could but to bring little pieces of it back to his family to make up for causing them to miss out on it themselves.

What if he had it wrong?

He'd never asked himself that question before. Why was he asking it now?

Before he'd finished forming the thought, the answer came to him.

The woman who walked beside him.

Abby.

An unfamiliar feeling stirred in his heart.

She made him think and feel things he'd never considered before. He'd known from the beginning that she was different from the usual women he went out with, but after making love to her all last night, he was more sure of it than ever.

No strings attached had been his motto, and in the light of day those strings got tangled. But waking up with Abby in his arms had been different. It had been right. Natural.

And the sex had been mind-blowing. Abby was a verbal lover. She'd gasped, cried out, and moaned. Nearly driven him over the edge. She'd shuddered beneath his sensual caresses. Had dug her nails into his back. Kissed him with a passion that matched his own. Her response to his touch made him even more eager to please her.

But in direct contrast to her passion, she had an innocence about her that he found irresistible. It brought out an unusual urge in him to protect and care for her.

Lovemaking aside, he'd enjoyed exploring the various islands and attractions they'd found at each port of call. She'd been so excited about the things they'd discovered at each stop. She made him see the world in a different way, in more ways than one.

But he also loved walking with her. Like now. He couldn't think of anyone else he'd rather pretend to be married to.

Noah ignored the voice in the back of his mind that told him making love to her had made it all too real.

He looked over at her, where she ambled beside him in the surf. The sun had dried most of the water clinging to her, but droplets fell from the ends of her long, wet hair onto her shoulders. Noah had the sudden urge to lick those drops away. He could almost taste the saltiness on his tongue.

Seeming to sense his gaze on her, Abby glanced over and smiled. "It's beautiful, isn't it?" She raised her face to the sky, as if inviting the warmth of the day to caress her face.

"Yes." His answer was for the woman walking next to him, however, rather than the endless stretch of sand and sky ahead of them. Her skin had taken on a bronzed glow from their recent days in the sun, and her paisley patterned bikini exposed much of it to his view. The bottom clung to the curve of her hip and rode low on her stomach, calling attention to the flat plane of her abdomen. The top of the suit cupped her full breasts and tied around the back of her neck. His body hardened at the sight of her nipples poking through the thin fabric.

He remembered her instant response when he'd taken them in his mouth the night before. In his mind he heard again the soft sounds she'd made in the back of her throat as he'd enticed the buds into hard peaks with flicks of his tongue.

He groaned, not realizing the sound had carried until Abby turned questioning eyes on him.

"Let—" He stopped, clearing his throat when his voice cracked. "Let's walk up that way for a little while." He indicated a group of rocks that jutted out from the upper portion of the beach.

"Sure." Abby followed along as he tugged on her hand.

They had walked far enough away from the crowd dotting the beach near the cabanas, so that they were virtually alone. He led Abby around the rocks, making their privacy complete. Satisfied they were truly alone, he pulled her into his arms and rocked his hips against hers.

"Oh my," she breathed. Her eyes grew wide. The pupils dilated.

His mouth captured hers. Stroking. Seeking. He increased the pressure when he felt her response, but forced himself to kiss her slowly, taking his time, despite the fact that the soft mewling sounds she made in the back of her throat had him straining for release.

Never breaking the kiss, he lowered her to the sand, followed her down, and pinned her body with his own.

Chapter Thirteen

The welcome weight of Noah's body pressed Abby into the hot sand, the grains rough beneath her back. Her hands grasped his sun-warmed shoulders, pulling him to her as he deepened the kiss. His tongue stroked against hers, and liquid heat pooled between her thighs.

He smelled of sun and sand and water, the combination intoxicating. That and the illicitness of being out in the open, on the beach, with the wide expanse of blue sky overhead. Sexual adrenalin poured through her. Her entire body flushed with a desire that far surpassed the heat of the day.

Noah's mouth left hers to blaze a trail of hot kisses down her arched neck. He nipped her collarbone and licked the water droplets from her shoulders. He moved to her breast and took the nipple in his mouth, sucking it through the damp fabric of her swimsuit. She arched off the sand, pushing herself further into the heat of his mouth.

Noah used the movement to slip his hands beneath her and untie her top. He drew it away from her body in his teeth, which freed his hands to wander over her exposed skin. They cupped her breasts, his fingertips brushing over the sensitive tips. Her breath hitched, and she bit her lip to keep from crying out as he continued the sensual torture.

Unable to lie passive beneath him, she skimmed her hands over his shoulders and down his back until she reached the waistband of his shorts. She slid beneath the fabric, pushing him deeper into the juncture of her spread thighs. The thin barrier of their swimsuits was no match for the hard steel of Noah's arousal. He pressed against her. Hot and hard.

Bracing most of his weight on his arms, he moved against her. The movement, enhanced by the erotic friction of their clothing, started a delicate shiver of trembling between her legs. Her eyes flew open, locking onto the deep blue of Noah's. He continued the purposeful thrust of his hips.

The trembling increased.

Her hands clutched at his shoulders. Her hips lifted and writhed against him.

"Noah," she managed on a gasp. "Please, I..." But she didn't know what she was pleading for. She didn't want him to stop, but if he kept going she was going to—

"Oh." Her voice shook.

"Yes." Noah's unsteady voice whispered across her skin. "That's it. Let go, Abby."

His head lowered to her breast, and he took the tip into his mouth. He drew on the tight nipple. His tongue stroked over it once before she shattered. Molten heat coursed through her veins. The spasms of fire raced along her nerves. She shuddered against Noah as he cupped her hip in his hand, pressing her body even closer to his.

The trembling waves of pleasure seemed to go on forever, but gradually she returned to herself. She panted as she lay beneath him. Her gaze met his. Deep satisfaction glowed in his eyes.

"I—"

"I know." He brought his mouth down on hers.

Still dazed, Abby kissed him, then moved away. Noah looked at her with questioning eyes, but she smiled, pushing against his chest until he lay on his back beside her. She leaned over him, propped on one elbow. She ran her palm across his chest, then down over the fabric covering his straining arousal.

His hips arched, and she favored him with another smile. "Now it's your turn," she whispered.

His eyes widened.

She rained kisses across his shoulders. The muscles tensed beneath her lips as she kissed her way down his chest, but he lay passive beneath her. His breath caught when she reached the waistband of his suit. She licked a salty drop of water from his navel, lingered a moment, then kissed her way back up his chest. She slid her hand beneath his shorts. He jerked.

She stroked him, gently at first, reveling in the groan that escaped from between his clenched teeth. Her mouth opened against the base of his throat and found the rapid beat of his pulse. She laved it with her tongue.

His breath came in short pants as she stroked harder. He quivered and strained against her palm. She ran her thumb over the tip of him, spreading the bead of moisture there. His hips rocked again. He reached down to grab her hand in his.

"Stop." The word was harsh. Grating.

"But I want—"

"I want to be inside you."

The words, accompanied by the unsteady tone of his voice, sent a thrill of excitement through Abby. He raised his hips, skimming his swim shorts off, then hooked a finger beneath the waist of her suit bottom and dragged it down her legs.

Still prone, he pulled her over him so she straddled his waist, then lowered her onto his body until she took the full length of him inside her. Her head fell back, and she gasped at the intense pleasure. She remained still for long moments, savoring the feel of him hot, hard, and pulsing inside her, before she moved.

He let her set the pace as she rose and fell above him. His hands guided her hips as his own lifted to meet hers and then fall away. She leaned forward, bracing her hands on his shoulders. As the tremors began deep inside her once again, she moved faster.

With a shudder that wracked her entire body, Abby collapsed against Noah, falling onto his chest, as he thrust into her one final time. His hands tightened on her as release claimed him as well. His cry echoed off the nearby rocks, the sound bouncing around them for endless moments as the sensual vibrations in her body peaked, then drained away.

She lay over him, the rapid rise and fall of his chest beneath hers, the harsh sound of his breathing in her ear. Her own breath was erratic, and it took a while before she could draw a deep gulp of air into her lungs.

She allowed her body to separate from his, feeling the loss as he slid out of her. He snuggled her next to him, his arm around her, her hand resting on his chest over his heart.

In time the rapid beat slowed to a normal rhythm.

She lay entwined on the sand with him, her head nestled on his shoulder, tracing her hand down his chest and side, feeling the indentation of each rib. His hand stroked her shoulder.

She wanted to stay as they were for eternity. Loving the warmth of the sun shining down on them. Loving the heat of his body next to hers. Loving the way his fingers whispered across her skin.

Loving him.

No matter what the future held, Noah held a piece of her heart no other man would ever claim. Without a doubt the memory of their erotic lovemaking on the beach would always haunt her soul.

After a long while, Noah shifted. "We should probably be heading back." He sounded reluctant.

Abby nodded, but didn't move. Heading back meant returning to reality, and she wasn't ready to do that yet. Soon, reality would be returning to a life without Noah. She didn't want to think about that, so she lay still, letting the feel of being tangled up with him on the sand under a wide, Caribbean sky burn itself into her memory.

She'd never forget this moment for as long as she lived.

Noah stirred again. She sat up. Behind her he rose to his feet in an easy, fluid motion. He slid his swim trunks back on, and she wriggled into her bottoms, stood, then held her hair out of the way so he could retie her top.

"I liked it better when I was taking this off." He kissed the curve of her neck where it met her shoulder.

She laughed and turned to face him. His hands dropped to her waist. Her arms rose to wrap around his neck as he lowered his lips to hers. The kiss was sweet and tender and all too short.

He pulled away and took her hand without a word as they walked back toward the cabanas at the other end of the beach, a little bit closer to reality.

****

The next day was their last on the ship, and they were at sea with no ports of call. Abby found it ironic in a melancholy way to remember the beginning of the trip. She had been wishing for it to be over, and now she was desperate to hold onto these last precious moments with Noah. She couldn't believe how things had changed in five short days.

They spent most of the day in bed, emerging only to head down to the dining room for dinner when their hungry bodies demanded another kind of satisfaction. After a final filming session with the representatives from the TV show, they headed back to their cabin.

Not wanting to leave it until the last minute, Abby tossed what she could into her suitcase, leaving out only what she'd need in the morning.

As she folded one of her sundresses, a small package fell onto the bedspread. A cold knot twisted her insides.

The earrings she'd bought for Claire.

She sank onto the bed, clutching the bag in her hand. She hadn't thought about Claire in days.

Guilt flooded through her.

Everything Abby had tried to convince Claire of had become a lie. The rumpled and twisted sheets around her taunted her with the proof of her betrayal.

Claire would never forgive her now.

A lone tear slipped down her cheek. Another followed until they streamed uncontrollably down her face.

Somewhere deep inside she knew she had to pull herself together. She didn't want to ruin her last night with Noah by crying.

But then he knelt before her. "Abby, sweetheart, what's the matter? Why are you crying?"

The concern in his voice started a fresh avalanche of tears. "I...I..." Her voice trembled. She sucked in a shuddering breath.

"Okay, shhhhh," he murmured as he rose from his knees and then pulled her into his arms. He rested against the headboard and cuddled her while she cried.

She cried for her lost friendship with Claire. She cried for the lie she'd been living for the past week. She cried for her last night here with Noah.

But most of all she cried for the beautiful feelings in her heart she'd never be able to share with him.

After the tears subsided, she lay quietly, listening to the steady thud of his heart beneath her ear.

What did he think of her now? Had she ruined their last night together?

She took a deep breath.

"Better?" He kissed the top of her head.

She nodded. A good cry always did make her feel better. "I'm sorry."

"For what?"

"I didn't want you to see me like that."

"There's nothing to be sorry for. It's been an...emotional week."

"Yes." Then, although he didn't press further, she continued. "I...I found the earrings I bought for Claire."

The hand stroking her back paused a moment before continuing its soothing motion. "Ah."

"I lied to her," she whispered.

Noah sighed. "You didn't lie to her."

She pushed out of his embrace. "Didn't I? I told her that none of this was real. I told her I didn't want you. And then we—"

"Abby, listen to me. We didn't plan this. It just happened."

"If she knew..."

"Are you going to tell her?"

"No, but—"

"Neither am I. She'll never find out. She doesn't need to know. What happened between us is exactly that. Between us."

He was right. Claire could never know. It would kill her.

Abby nodded.

"Look at me."

She raised her eyes to his.

"We didn't do anything wrong." He kissed her softly.

A kiss so gentle and sweet that fresh moisture sprang to her eyes.

"Do you feel how right this is? Don't make it wrong," he whispered against her lips.

Whereas the beach had been erotic and decadent, their lovemaking that night was tender, yet urgent. The next day they'd go their separate ways, and she would have only the memory of their time together to hold close at night. As she held Noah to her as he moved in her and with her, she closed her eyes and tried to make the moment last as long as possible.

Morning would come all too soon.

****

Noah awoke sometime later. Abby lay curled against him, her back pressed to his chest, her legs tangled with his. Not wanting to disturb her, but unable to help himself, he pressed a kiss to her nape, inhaling the sweet fragrance of her hair as he nuzzled her neck.

She stirred. "What time is it?" she murmured.

He glanced at the digital clock on the television across the room. "Just after three. Go back to sleep."

She rolled onto her back and looked up at him. He couldn't make out the color of her eyes in the shadowy, moonlit room, but could imagine their deep green shade.

"I didn't mean to wake you."

Her hand rose to stroke his jaw. He turned his head and placed a kiss against her palm, then moved his lips to the gold band encircling the third finger on her left hand.

Had it really been less than a week since he'd placed it there? In less than a day their fake marriage would be over.

Suddenly, although he couldn't explain why, it was important that it didn't end yet. He wasn't through pretending.

"Come on." He slid out from beneath the sheet.

"What?" The husky note of her sleep slurred

voice whispered over him like a caress.

"Let's go outside."

Abby sat up. "Now?"

"I want to look at the stars with you." He tugged her hand, and she rose to follow him.

He pulled the sheet from the bed, then led her out onto the balcony. He stood behind her and wrapped his arms around her waist, draping them both in the soft cotton.

She leaned back against him, resting her head on his shoulder. He rubbed her cheek with his own. She turned her face toward him and raised her lips to his. His mouth touched hers for a brief kiss.

"Look." He pointed. Millions of stars dotted the heavens above them. Even the light from the full moon couldn't diminish their brilliance. The orb hung low in the sky, casting a silvery, glittering reflection on the rolling waves of the water below.

She snuggled back against him with a contented sigh. "It's breathtaking," she whispered. "You never see this at home."

He kissed her temple. A soft breeze blew a tendril of lilac-scented hair across his cheek. It caught on the stubble of his unshaven jaw.

He'd seen stars all over the world, but none as spectacular as these. Holding Abby in his arms while he gazed at the wonder above him made the sight even more beautiful.

She pressed closer beneath the sheet, her hip grazing him. He hardened.

"Noah," she murmured.

He shifted their positions. "Later," he promised. For now he wanted to hold her in his arms. Nothing more.

He rested his chin on the top of her head as they both gazed up at the sky. A shooting star streaked across the vast expanse.

"Did you see that?" Excitement laced her voice.

"Mmm, hmmmm." He kissed the shell of her ear, pleased when she shivered against him. "Make a wish." He waited, then asked, "What did you wish for?"

Abby laughed. "I can't tell you, silly, it won't come true." She turned to look up at him. "Did you make one?"

Noah looked into her eyes. "Mine already came true." His lips claimed hers.

She turned into his embrace and melted into the kiss. The sheet fell to the deck at their feet. This time he didn't ignore the demands of his body. He tilted his hips and pressed his arousal against her.

"Is it later?" Her mouth barely moved under his.

He swept her into his arms. "Oh, yes."

He placed her on the bed, then looked down at her, memorizing the perfect contours of her body, bathed in the pale moonlight streaming through the open balcony door. Her passion-filled eyes gazed back at him.

He smiled and ran his fingertips down the side of her face. Her silky smooth skin was hot beneath his touch. He trailed his fingers down her throat, between the valley of her breasts, to her waist. Using both hands, he turned her over to reveal the smooth expanse of her back.

With one finger, he traced down her spine. She shivered beneath his light touch. His hand trembled as he brushed her hair to the side. He leaned in to press a moist, hot kiss to the nape of her neck.

A breathy sigh escaped her lips.

He kissed his way down her spine. When he reached the concave curve below her waist, he brushed his lips back and forth. His hands tightened on her hips, holding her in place, as she twisted beneath his mouth.

His tongue traced back up her spine.

Her sigh turned to a moan.

He turned her again, then covered her mouth with his own.

Her hands feathered across his shoulders as he kissed his way down her throat. When he flicked his tongue over the tip of her breast, her nails dug into him.

The slight abrasion sent a burning fissure of desire through him. He pulled more deeply on her nipple, then sucked on the flesh at the top of her breast.

He wanted to brand her as his own one more time. Leave his mark on her.

Her hands slid down his back, then around to his stomach. She moved lower.

He corralled her hands in one of his. "Oh, no. Not yet." His voice shook. If she touched him like she had yesterday on the beach, he'd lose control. And he wasn't done yet.

"It's still my turn," he murmured as he drew her hands over her head.

He kissed her wrist, his lips brushing over the bracelet he'd placed there. Days ago. A different lifetime ago. A time before he'd made her his wife in every sense of the word.

He moved down her arm, stopping to suck on the soft skin at the inside of her elbow. Her hands twisted in his grasp, but he didn't let her go.

When he reached her shoulder, he nuzzled the side of her neck, then ran his tongue back and forth along the ridge of her collarbone.

She released a shuddery sigh.

He traced a finger around her breast, narrowing the circles until he reached the crest. The nipple hardened, as if in anticipation of his touch.

When he brushed over the tightened bud, she jerked beneath his touch. Short gasps tore from her throat. The beat of his heart matched the rapid pace of her uneven breaths.

He slid a fraction of an inch closer to losing control.

His hand moved to her stomach. His finger outlined her navel before dipping inside. He moved lower.

She squirmed beneath him, once again twisting her hands to free them from his grasp. He allowed her to pull free.

Her hand grasped his wrist. "No." The word came out hoarse.

He stilled and raised his eyes to hers.

"I want to feel you inside me."

At the bold words, an echo of his own on the beach, the rigid control he'd had on himself snapped.

With a growl he reached for a packet on the nightstand.

"Open your eyes," he commanded when he turned back to her.

She obeyed. Unfulfilled desire swam in their depths, visible even in the dim light. Passion. For him.

"I want you to look in your husband's eyes while he makes love to you." He didn't question the words. For now they were right. One last time, he would make love to his wife.

He grasped her leg, pulling it over his hip. She hooked her calf around his knee. In one smooth motion, he slid into her.

She tightened around him, drawing him deeper into her honeyed warmth.

When he moved, she matched her rhythm to his. With each stroke, he pressed further, wanting to touch the deepest part of her.

Much too soon, for he wanted the moment to go on, her release claimed her. She pulsed around him as tiny shivers wracked her body. Even as her body trembled beneath him, her eyes stayed locked on his.

And then his own release crashed over him.

****

Abby woke, nestled against Noah, to sunlight streaming in through the partially open balcony door. She lay still, her back pressed against his chest, cherishing the last precious moments in the arms of the man she loved. Once he awoke, it would all be over.

Noah would go back to his adventures, and she would go back to her predictable, well-planned, orderly life. A few days ago the thought would have thrilled her, but now life as before held little appeal. Any life without Noah held little appeal.

But life with Noah wasn't an option, so she held still, hardly daring to breathe, lest she disturb him. She wanted to savor this last contact for the longest possible time.

All too soon Noah stirred. His arms tightened, and he kissed her neck. She rolled onto her back and looked up at him as he lay on his side next to her, his head propped on his hand.

For endless heartbeats they stared at one another. Without breaking the silence, Abby tried to tell him how much the past week had meant to her. Whether he understood the silent communication or not, she'd never know.

He kissed her. The sweet intensity of it brought tears to her eyes. He opened his mouth to say something, but she placed a finger against his lips.

"Don't," she whispered.

Noah nodded, taking long moments to pull his gaze from hers, then slid out from beneath the covers.

She closed her eyes, not willing to watch him go.

They went through the motions of the morning like polite acquaintances rather than the lovers they'd been for the last few days.

While she finished packing, she found the blue pendant Noah had given her to wear on their wedding day. The one all the Grant brides wore. Tears filled her eyes and blurred her vision. With trembling fingers she replaced it in the box, then turned to Noah.

"Here." She held it out to him. "I didn't realize I still had this."

He took the small box, looking at it before his eyes met hers. "Thanks. And thank you for wearing it."

She nodded, then swallowed twice before she managed to respond. "You're welcome."

Her packing complete, she placed a sorely neglected Annie on top of the clothes before shutting the suitcase. She couldn't believe it had come to this.

They were about to leave the cabin to begin the disembarkation process, when Noah stopped. Closing the door, he turned to her. "Abby, I think we should talk."

"No." She wouldn't be able to bear it. "It's better this way. Please," she added when he didn't waver. She took a fortifying breath. "We need to be out on deck."

With obvious reluctance, Noah nodded. "Yeah. Sure. Let's get going."

The film crew from the television studio wasn't recording the end of their trip. The interview at sunset the night before would close out the show once it aired. Which was good. She doubted she could muster a smile, even a false one, when her heart was breaking.

Getting off the ship went smoothly, and soon they sat on a plane heading home. A limousine took them from the airport to her house.

And then it was over.

They waited in her living room for Noah's cab to arrive. They didn't talk. Abby didn't know what to say to him anymore. Had it only been that morning that she'd woken in his arms after a night of lovemaking? It seemed like a lifetime ago.

Finally his cab honked.

"Well, I guess this is it."

She hugged herself. "Yeah." She avoided looking at him.

"Abby." Her name came out soft, like a caress.

He stepped closer, framed her face in his hands, and raised it up, forcing her to meet his gaze. His eyes probed hers. Then he smiled.

Another piece of her heart broke.

"I had fun."

At that she had to smile. "Yeah, me too."

"I'll never forget this."

"Me either."

His head lowered, and she gave in to one more kiss. One final good-bye kiss to last her through the lonely years ahead. She fought back the tears that threatened as his lips moved against hers. She'd have time to cry later.

Noah broke the contact, brushing one last kiss across her forehead before stepping back. His hands fell to his sides.

She clasped hers in front of her to quell the urge to reach out to him.

He gathered his bags. At the door he turned. "I'll call you in a couple of days so we can figure out what we need to do."

The annulment. A fresh wave of pain stabbed at her, but she nodded. "Okay."

He opened the door and stepped through. "Good-bye, Abby."

And then he was gone.

Chapter Fourteen

Mr. and Mrs. Noah Grant.

The words shouted at Abby from the large
manila envelope in her hand. She glanced at the
address label. The package had come from the
television studio that had filmed the game show and
their wedding. She wanted to know what was inside,
but at the same time was reluctant to open it.

Finally she turned it over and ran a fingernail
underneath the closure at one end. Tipping the
envelope, she dumped the contents out on her
kitchen table. A DVD, another smaller, thick
envelope, and a letter fell out.

Ignoring the disc and the envelope, she reached
for the letter. She skipped over the part
congratulating her and Noah on their recent
marriage until she found an explanation for the
other items. The DVD held a preview of the show
that would air in a couple of months, and the
envelope held pictures from their trip.

She sank onto one of the kitchen chairs and
contemplated the envelope for a full five minutes
before reaching for it. It took another five minutes to
gather the courage to open it. The large stack of
photographs weighted down her hand.

Then, one at a time, she flipped through them. A
photo chronology of her marriage and honeymoon
with Noah. The sight of him smiling out at her from
the pictures sent a pang straight to her heart. It had
been more than two weeks since they'd returned
from their trip.

He'd called a day or two after they'd gotten back

to let her know he'd be out of town to catch up on work. A quick trip to New York. It had been odd, hearing his voice through the tinny filter of her answering machine. But she wasn't surprised he was back in the swing of things, jetting off to someplace new.

He'd said he'd call her again when he returned and after he'd talked to his lawyer.

She didn't have to guess what that meant. He needed to talk about their annulment. At the start of all of this, it had sounded so simple. Get married. Take a great vacation. Get an annulment.

Easy.

Now those words held a whole new meaning. Being married to Noah wasn't something she could easily throw away.

Her gaze fell on the silver bracelet adorning her right wrist. She hadn't taken it off. More so than the wedding band encircling the third finger of her left hand, the bracelet provided a bittersweet reminder of their time together. The wedding band acted as a prop provided by the television studio as part of their prize. But the bracelet had come from Noah. He'd chosen it for her, and that had touched a little bit of her soul, even before she'd fallen in love with him, by the gesture and the sweet words he'd spoken. About commitment.

Soon their legal commitment would end.

An annulment sounded so harsh, so unreal. Not a simple thing at all, but a thing that caused waves of pain to crash over her whenever she thought about it.

Not easy at all.

The nights were the hardest. She missed the breeze blowing off the Gulf into her room. She missed the gentle, almost imperceptible sway of the ship rocking her to sleep. Most of all she missed Noah.

She lay awake at night, longing for the feel of his arms around her, the feel of his lips brushing across the back of her neck as they lay curled together.

A tear slipped down her cheek and blurred the images in front of her. She wiped the moisture away, unwilling to let anything impair the sight of him, even if only in a picture, when her heart longed for him.

They looked so happy. Had they really smiled at one another so much? Had they really held hands all the time? There was hardly a picture in the pile where they weren't touching in some way. For all intents and purposes, they looked like a couple very much in love.

Which is what they had set out to do at the beginning of everything. Make it look as real as possible. Judging from the pictures in front of her, they had accomplished their goal.

Except for her it had become real. She'd fallen in love with Noah.

Her hands trembled as she flipped through the stack of pictures once more. She stared at yet another image of him smiling out at her and let the tears come, until she could no longer see his face.

****

Noah stood in his darkroom and looked around, not quite able to believe what he saw.

After returning from a business trip, which had been disturbingly unsatisfying, he had itched to get into his darkroom. Not to develop pictures from his recent trip, but to develop the photographs he'd taken on his vacation with Abby.

Now here he was, surrounded by images of her. He'd gotten some great shots of the scenery in the places they had been, but most of it provided a backdrop for the figure that dominated all of them.

In one her hair was tumbled by the breeze. His

fingers itched to feel the silken texture. In another she smiled teasingly at him from behind a palm tree. His mouth hungered for the taste of her. In yet another she stood silhouetted against the crumbling ruins at Tulum, right before she'd fallen and twisted her ankle. The memory of the pain in her eyes tugged at his heart.

A hundred more images surrounded him. Teasing. Taunting. Evoking sweet, erotic memories.

He shook his head to clear it.

Through the closed door, the sound of the ringing phone reached him. He didn't bother trying to answer it. The machine would pick up.

The disembodied voice on the answering machine filtered in to him. His lawyer. Letting him know the paperwork to end his marriage was ready. The document needed to be signed to make it official.

Noah sighed, once again looking at the images around him. He needed to call Abby and let her know.

****

"Abby told us you met through a mutual friend. What was your first impression of her?"

Abby's heart pinched as she watched Noah contemplate the question. Reminders of Claire always made her heart hurt. Claire still hadn't returned any of her phone calls. Abby had called her as soon as they'd returned from the trip and several times after, but Claire never called back. And although Abby missed her, part of her didn't know what to say to her. How could she tell her best friend she'd fallen in love with Noah?

What would Claire say if she ever found out how real it had become?

If missing Claire made her heart ache, missing Noah made her feel as if her heart was gone. His image filled the TV screen in her living room. He looked real enough to touch. She ached to touch him.

One more time.

Against her better judgment, she'd slipped the DVD from the studio into the player. She hadn't been able to stop herself. Like an addict, she'd needed her fix. It had been forever since she'd seen him. Touched him. Tasted him.

At least it felt that way.

She'd never asked what he'd said during his interview in Cozumel. Now she was going to find out.

On the screen, Noah answered the question Sandy had posed. "Well, she's beautiful, of course. But, as cliché as it sounds, she's even more beautiful on the inside."

"What do you love the most about Abby?"

The question caused her heart to squeeze again. She remembered how odd it had been to talk about being in love with Noah when she'd given her interview. That had been before she'd realized she *did* love him.

What would he say? Would she be able to bear hearing him talk about loving her? Could she stand the lie?

"What's not to love? She's the kindest, sweetest, most genuine person I've ever met."

Abby blinked back tears. He made the lies sound so sincere. No one else watching would ever guess he'd been making it up as he went along.

"Abby said you were romantic."

"She did?" Noah sounded pleased at the thought.

Abby had to give him credit. He was good.

Sandy nodded. "What's the most romantic thing you've ever done for her? Or better yet, what would *she* say is the most romantic thing you've ever done?"

Noah smiled. Abby's heart skittered.

"Oh, that's easy. On our wedding day I gave her a pendant that belonged to my great-grandma. Abby would have thought that was very romantic. She's very traditional."

Abby stared at the TV screen in shock. How could Noah have possibly known her so well? He was dead on. She'd given virtually the same answer during her interview. And they hadn't even rehearsed that one.

On the screen, Sandy smiled at Noah. "Abby said the same thing. About the pendant."

Noah raised an eyebrow. "Really?" Again, pleasure tinged his voice.

"You two really are perfect for each other."

Abby grimaced. Noah wouldn't have an answer for that.

"So," Sandy continued. "How, then, did you two wind up getting married on TV because of a game show? That doesn't seem very traditional."

Noah grinned. "The whole game show thing was my idea. I thought it would be fun."

Abby smiled to herself. Was she the only one who would hear the slight emphasis he'd put on the word *fun*?

"Abby went along with the whole thing. She was a real trouper. Of course, I don't think she ever dreamed we'd win."

Understatement of the year.

"But, hey, a sunset wedding on the beach? It doesn't get much more romantic than that," Noah concluded.

"What's been the best part of the trip so far?"

"Spending it with Abby." He smiled again, this time with a touch of self-deprecation. "I know, I know. I'm sounding cliché again." He ran his fingers through his hair.

Abby's heart tightened at the familiar gesture.

"But really. I travel all over the world for my job. It's great. I love it. I've seen some really amazing things. Things most people won't ever experience in their lifetime. But what makes this trip special is that I'm sharing it with her."

"She's a lucky woman."

Was it her imagination, or could Abby actually hear the undertone of wistfulness in the other woman's tone? Or was it that she'd heard Sandy express her appreciation of Noah firsthand?

An unexpected knot of jealousy twisted her insides. Was Sandy the kind of woman Noah would normally go for?

Of course he would. Gorgeous. Blonde. And obviously interested.

She shook the feeling off. The interview had been given weeks ago. A lifetime ago. It didn't matter.

Besides, she had no claim on Noah. Their days of pretending were over. He probably was back to dating by now.

She swallowed the painful lump in her throat.

"No, I'm the lucky one," Noah insisted.

Abby returned her attention to the screen.

"Well, then what happens next for you two?"

Abby braced herself for the lie to come. Nothing came next.

Not for her and Noah.

He shrugged. "The future is always full of surprises. It's a constant adventure. I'm just glad that I've finally found someone to share my adventures with."

Abby listened to the conclusion of Noah's interview, then through a haze of tears, hit the still button on the remote.

She stared at Noah's face, frozen on the screen.

The video was worse than the pictures had been. Especially the clips where they'd talked about their feelings. Even knowing it was all made up, the words Noah had said about her had her falling even more in love with him. Watching as the wedding and the rest of the trip unfolded, no one would ever guess that they had been reluctant participants. They had both played their parts to the hilt.

Now the show was over, and they both needed to get back to reality. She supposed Noah was already back, off resuming the life he'd led before everything had happened. And here she was, trying to resume her life as before, but finding it difficult to do.

Sitting still no longer interested her. She didn't have a desire to traverse the world again like she had as a child, but a fun adventure every now and then didn't sound too bad.

Trouble was, she doubted she'd ever have an adventure like she'd had with Noah. Her husband. Nothing could match that once-in-a-lifetime experience.

How she wished the words he'd spoken were true. Sharing adventures with him would make her future perfect. But it wasn't meant to be.

She aimed the remote at the TV. His image faded.

Soon he'd fade from her life, and she'd be left with only the memories of their time together.

She had to forget about him and move on. And hope that one day Claire would be able to forgive her. The best thing to do would be to throw all of the pictures in the trash and use the DVD for a hot plate or a coaster.

She couldn't make herself do it. She would keep the mementoes of their time together for the rest of her life. As she'd keep a piece of him in her heart for that long as well.

She jumped when the phone on the end table rang.

"Hello?"

"Abby? It's Noah."

She savored the sound of the deep timbre of his voice. She'd missed it over the last few weeks.

"Abby? Are you there?"

"I'm here."

This time there was a pause at his end of the line. Then, "How are you?"

"I'm fine," she lied. "How was your trip?"

"Okay."

"Just okay?"

"Yeah. Um, anyway, the reason I'm calling is I, uh, heard from my lawyer, and he has the papers ready for us to sign."

Tears clogged her throat. She swallowed, forcing them back. She wouldn't let him hear her cry. "Oh. Okay."

Another long silence descended on the line.

Finally Noah spoke. "Would it be okay if I came by later this week to drop them off?"

"Sure," she said, although it was the last thing she wanted.

"How about Thursday?"

"Tha—" She cleared her throat. "That should be fine. I'll be home after work."

"Okay. I guess I'll see you then?"

"Sure." She hung up the phone.

She hugged herself, feeling sick to her stomach. The awkward conversation replayed itself in her mind. Gone was the carefree intimacy they'd shared. They no longer spoke like lovers, but like casual acquaintances. Ones that weren't quite sure what to say to each other.

How could everything have changed so quickly? As if nothing had ever passed between them. The reality she'd feared had returned with a vengeance.

Still feeling queasy, she rose from the sofa, then headed to the kitchen to find some ginger ale to settle her stomach.

The feeling worsened the next day. She got a call from the television studio inviting her and Noah to a special charity dinner in conjunction with the show. They were to be the guests of honor.

They'd have to find a way to get out of it. She couldn't handle another night of Noah pretending to be in love with her.

Maybe he'd be out of town.

She called, but crossed her fingers. Maybe his answering machine would pick up.

"Hello?"

No such luck.

She rushed on. "I thought maybe you were out of town again."

"Nope."

"Oh."

"You sound disappointed." Through the phone his teasing voice tickled her senses.

"No, it's not that. The television studio called, and they want us to attend this charity thing, and I thought we could get out of it if you were out of town, but I'll make something else up and—"

"I think we should go."

"What?"

"I mean," Noah hesitated. "For appearance sake, we should probably make an effort to be there."

"I suppose," Abby said. Why did Noah sound almost eager to go?

"When is it?"

"Wednesday night."

Another pause. She heard him shuffling some papers. "Great, I'm free that night. I'll pick you up at six forty-five."

She hung up the phone.

Another night with Noah.

Pretending to be husband and wife.

Her heart couldn't take it.

****

When the phone rang Wednesday afternoon, Abby rushed to answer it, hoping against hope Noah was calling to say something had come up, and he

177

couldn't make it to dinner after all.

"Hi. It's Claire."

After weeks of silence, the unexpected sound of her friend's voice took her by surprise. "Hi." Abby didn't know what else to say.

"Um, how are you?"

Not good. But she couldn't share her feelings about Noah with Claire.

"I'm okay."

"Good, I mean, that's great."

The stilted, awkward conversation saddened Abby. They'd always been able to talk so easily. But at least they were talking. Claire had called her. She'd take that as a good sign.

"Look, I was wondering if you wanted to get together tonight. Do drinks or something."

Abby's heart brightened. At last Claire wanted to talk.

Then it sank. She had to go to dinner tonight. With Noah.

"Oh, Claire, I'd love to, but I can't tonight, Noah and I—"

"You're going out with Noah?" Claire's voice accused.

Abby cursed to herself. "No, it's not like that. We—"

"I thought the TV show was it. I didn't realize you two were dating."

"It was. We're not," Abby assured her. She forced away the pain the words brought. "The TV station is having some charity dinner, and they want us there."

"Oh." Claire didn't sound convinced.

"Really, that's all it is. Some publicity thing. I'd rather be going out for drinks with you." No lie there. "What about tomorrow night?"

"I can't tomorrow."

"Oh. Well, then maybe some other time soon?"

"Sure," Claire agreed, but she didn't sound thrilled with the idea.

"I'll call you." Abby tried to keep the sadness out of her voice.

"Sure," Claire said again. "I've got to go." She hung up.

Abby placed the phone in its cradle.

Would things ever be right with Claire again? Abby had hoped that given enough time Claire would forgive her and come around.

That didn't seem to be happening. Now it would be worse since Claire knew Abby would be seeing Noah again tonight.

The doorbell rang promptly at six forty-five. Abby steeled herself and opened the door to see Noah's smiling face.

"Hi," she managed over the painful thump of her heart. Funny how she didn't know what else to say to the man standing before her.

The man she loved.

The man she'd spent days making love to and being loved in return. At least in a physical sense.

"You look beautiful." He stepped across the threshold, then brushed her cheek with a kiss.

She closed her eyes as his lips whispered over her skin. The familiar scent of his aftershave washed over her.

She opened her eyes. "Thanks." She'd agonized over what to wear, but had decided on a simple black dress. Her gaze swept over the suit Noah wore with an open-necked shirt. No tie. On the cruise he'd worn casual shirts and shorts. She hadn't seen him in a suit since their wedding day.

She swallowed and pushed the thought aside. "You look nice too."

He grinned. "Are you ready to go?"

She grabbed her coat from the hook behind the door. "I'm set."

Before she could shrug her arms into the sleeves, Noah took the garment from her and held it out. She slipped it on. He settled it on her shoulders. His hands lingered. His breath stirred the tendrils of hair against her neck.

Even through layers of clothing, his touch sent a frisson of awareness through her. She stepped away.

From memories. From temptation.

"Let's get this show on the road," she said.

"One last act for old times sake, Mrs. Grant?" His tone teased, but the words stabbed into her.

"On that note," she said as they made their way toward the curb where his car sat, "you should have brought the annulment papers with you." The self-inflicted pain of her own words pushed the knife deeper. "It would have saved you another trip out here." She risked a glance at him.

The teasing light faded from his eyes, replaced by an emotion she couldn't interpret. He looked away. "Actually, I didn't have a chance to get to my lawyer's yet, so we'll have to take care of that next week."

"Oh, okay." She slid into the passenger side of the car. As he closed the driver's side door, she turned to him. "I'm sorry you got stuck with getting the paperwork ready. If there's anything I can do to help..."

"I'll take care of it." He sounded odd. "Don't worry."

"I'm not worried. I'm sure you want this over and done with as soon as possible." So did she. Maybe once the papers were signed, she'd be able to stop thinking about him.

They arrived at the studio right on time. Noah took her hand as they checked in with a security guard who escorted them through to the main studio. Dozens of round tables draped with white linen cloths crowded the soundstage. Elaborate floral and candle centerpieces graced the center of each table, and soft, classical music filled the air. Tuxedo-clad waiters circulated with trays laden with mini-quiches, shrimp, a variety of fruits and cheeses, and flutes of champagne.

"Fancy, shmancy." Noah leaned down to whisper in her ear.

Abby smiled up at him.

"Ah, Abby and Noah, there you are." The show's producer approached, his hand outstretched. He shook Noah's hand and kissed Abby's cheek. "How are my two favorite lovebirds?"

Abby winced.

"Just fine." Noah smiled. He tightened his fingers around hers and squeezed.

"I hope you kids enjoyed your honeymoon. Did you get the pictures we sent over?"

She nodded. "Yes, thank you."

"Everything turned out great. I'm sure you'll be pleased when the show airs." He glanced across the room. "I need to talk to someone. So glad you could make it." He hurried away.

Noah turned to her. "Pictures?"

"The studio sent a bunch of pictures and a DVD with a preview of the show."

"Did you watch it?" His light tone belied the serious expression in his eyes.

She hesitated. "Yes," she admitted, then changed the subject. "Do you want to find a place to sit and get something to drink?"

"Yeah, I could use a drink."

She raised an eyebrow at the cryptic words, but didn't comment.

They found an empty table and filled their plates with finger food from a passing waiter.

Abby picked at the mini quiche with her fork. She pushed her plate away without tasting any.

Being with Noah again was odd. The sound of

his voice as they chatted, the way his eyes crinkled when he smiled, the spicy scent of his aftershave as he leaned close, brought back sweet memories of their time on the ship.

And she couldn't get the conversation with Claire out of her mind.

"Abby, is something the matter?" Noah's voice broke into her musings. "You seem preoccupied."

"It's nothing."

"Maybe I can help."

She shook her head as she twirled the empty champagne glass between her fingers. "I don't think so. Claire called tonight and wanted to go out for drinks. It's the first time I've talked to her in ages. She got upset when I told her I couldn't because I had to be here with you." She glanced up and met Noah's gaze. "She hates me."

"I'm sure she doesn't hate you." He took her hand in his and stroked the back of it.

The familiar touch sent a shiver of desire through her. She still wanted him. Wanted to feel his touch everywhere, as she lay bare, next to the heat of his body.

She forced herself back to the topic at hand. Claire. They'd been talking about Claire. About how she wouldn't talk to her because of the man sitting across from her.

"I'm not so sure about that."

"Claire's a big girl. She'll be fine."

He'd said similar words before.

"Have you talked to her?"

He shook his head.

"Has she called you?"

"No. Why did you think she would?"

"I figured you and Claire would pick up where you left off. Before we...well, before all of this happened. I know that's what Claire would want."

"I can't see that happening. You really think

that's what she wants?"

Abby set the fragile glass down with a sharp thud on the table. "No, I don't. I used to know her. But I don't anymore. We don't talk."

"Whoa, easy, Abby, sweetheart."

The false endearment grated on her nerves.

She took a deep breath, then expelled it. "Sorry. I just thought we were done with all of this pretending, and now we had to do this tonight, and I just can't deal with—"

Noah cut her off. "Shhhhh." He twined his fingers with hers. "I'm sorry. I know all of this has been really hard on you. I didn't mean to sound like a jerk. But I want you to know," he paused, then continued when she lifted her eyes to his. "I'm not going to date Claire again. And I really am sorry that things got so messed up with the two of you."

"I know, I just wish..." She wanted to say she wished none of this had happened. But it would be a lie. For all the pain that was sure to come, she couldn't wish her time as Noah's wife away. The memories were already too precious.

She glanced at the matching wedding bands on their fingers. She hadn't taken hers off. Noah had probably put his back on for the night.

It had been far too easy tonight to slip back into their married routine. Far too easy to forget it was only part of the game.

****

After work the next day, the doorbell interrupted Abby on her way from the laundry room to her bedroom. She put the basket on the stairs, then retraced her steps back through the living room.

She opened the door. Claire stood on the doorstep.

"I bet you're surprised to see me." Claire offered a tentative smile. "I know I deserve to have you slam the door in my face, but I hope you won't. I'm sorry I've been such a bitch lately."

Abby laughed. Leave it to Claire to cut right to the chase.

Claire held up a pint of chocolate chip cookie dough ice cream. "I brought two spoons."

Abby smiled at the peace offering. She stepped aside to let her friend in. "Couch or kitchen?"

"Couch."

Abby sat at one end of the couch, crossing her legs beneath her. Claire assumed a similar position at the other end. She placed the tub of ice cream between them, then handed Abby a spoon.

She dipped it into the ice cream, then brought the heaping scoop to her mouth. She savored the creamy, coldness as it slid down her throat.

"Mmmmmm." Claire's appreciative murmur echoed Abby's own thoughts.

She looked over at her friend. "I've missed you."

"Me too."

"What made you finally decide to talk to me again?"

Claire frowned and shook her head. "I've been awful, haven't I?" Without waiting for a response, she continued, "Well, I was sitting at home last night feeling sorry for myself, thinking about you being out with Noah." She flashed an apologetic smile. "I turned on the TV and wouldn't you know it, about five minutes in, a commercial for Las Vegas came on. I couldn't believe it. And then I just started laughing.

"It felt good. And suddenly I wanted to be laughing with *you*. I wanted to laugh with you about all of this instead of acting like a moron. I realized that no matter what had happened, it wasn't worth ruining our friendship over. You mean much more to me than some guy."

Abby let the words settle into her bruised and

battered heart. As they washed through her, a part of her healed.

They polished off half the carton before Claire spoke again. "I'm sorry I've been acting so weird lately."

Abby shook her head. "You have every right to be upset."

"But did I have the right to treat you like I did? Not returning your calls? Accusing you of trying to steal Noah?"

Abby didn't know what to say to that. She couldn't honestly say she didn't understand the motivation behind Claire's actions, but they'd still hurt.

"I'm sorry," Claire continued. "Can you ever forgive me? I know I don't deserve your forgiveness after the way I've acted, but I've missed you like crazy, and I was hoping we could be friends again."

"We'll always be friends. We've always *been* friends."

"Even after all those awful things I said to you?"

Abby reached over to touch Claire's hand. "I know it was hard on you when Noah and I had to get married."

Claire nodded. "Noah and I weren't exclusive or anything, but when you told me you were getting married, it freaked me out."

"You and me both."

Claire laughed, then sobered. "I was jealous. The thought of you and Noah together drove me crazy." She paused. "Can I tell you something?"

"Of course."

"Promise you won't laugh?"

Abby made a crossing motion over her heart.

"At first, when I signed us up for that game show, it was a lark. I knew Noah wasn't the settling down type. I thought we could have had some fun, you know? I'm not a settling down kind of girl, and

Noah's not really a settling down kind of guy. That made him perfect for me."

Abby laughed to hide the pain Claire's words caused. No, Noah wasn't a settling down kind of guy at all. Which was why he wasn't perfect for her, no matter how much she loved him.

"But then," Claire continued, "I started thinking about what it would be like to win. To run off to Vegas and get married. To be totally spontaneous and adventurous. With Noah. I thought a lot about what it would be like to be married to Noah.

"And I liked the idea." She took a deep breath. "So, when I sprained my ankle and couldn't go, I wasn't willing to just forget the game show on the off chance that we might win. So I asked you to fill in for me. I figured you'd give me the prize if you won."

Abby's heart ached. She hadn't realized how much Claire had wanted to win.

Claire grimaced. "And then you guys came over and told me you did win. I couldn't believe it. In the back of my mind, I was packed and ready for Vegas. I could see Noah and me at one of those tacky little chapels there." She paused and looked at Abby. "And then you told me the rest of it."

"Oh, Claire. I didn't know. I—"

"Of course you didn't."

Abby remained silent for a moment, thinking about what Claire had told her. She swallowed. She needed to know something. "Do you still feel that way? About Noah?"

Claire smiled, but it was rueful. "To be honest, I don't think I ever felt that way about Noah. But I'd had this whole thing worked out in my mind, and then when I found out *you* were going to marry him, I totally lost it. I couldn't wrap my head around the idea of you two together. I knew it wasn't real, but it was hard to remember that. I couldn't stop thinking about the two of you."

Abby remained silent. What could she say?

"I know there's nothing going on. I know you would never do that."

Abby's heart squeezed. No, there wasn't anything going on anymore, but what would happen if Claire found out how real the honeymoon had been? Keeping secrets from her best friend wasn't something Abby made a habit of, but the real story of her time with Noah would remain one. She'd never be able to tell Claire she'd fallen in love with him. The thought saddened her.

Abby scraped the bottom of the cardboard carton with her spoon, collected the last of the ice cream, and slid it into her mouth. She wanted to ask Claire something else, but wasn't sure she had the courage.

After swallowing the ice cream, she took a deep breath. She studied the empty spoon in her hand, not looking at Claire. "So, do you think you'll see Noah again when all of this is over?" She tried to sound casual.

"What do you mean?"

"You know, do you think you'll start dating again?" Abby had no doubt Noah would date other women after their marriage ended, if he wasn't already, but the thought of him going back to Claire twisted her insides. Made her feel all inside-out.

He'd said he wouldn't date Claire again, but how did Claire feel about it? If she'd felt strongly enough about him to want to marry him, she'd probably want to see him again. If she called and asked him out would he change his mind?

Claire shook her head. "No, it would be too weird."

Abby hoped her relief didn't show. "I'm sorry things got messed up with you and Noah because of the game show and everything."

Claire shrugged. "That's okay. It wasn't meant to be." She tossed her spoon into the empty ice cream bucket. "So, what do you two do now?"

"Noah's getting the paperwork together for an annulment." Abby kept her voice neutral.

"You really have to go through all that legal stuff?"

"We had to get legally married, so now we have to get legally unmarried." Abby closed her heart to the ache the words brought.

"That sucks," Claire said.

"Yeah, it sure does." She forced a smile and hoped Claire couldn't see how false it was. "But, as soon as this is all over with, the sooner things can go back to normal." She paused. "Can I tell you something? Well, show you something?"

Claire looked puzzled. "Sure."

Abby uncurled her legs and rose. She grabbed the blue velvet jewelry box from the bookshelf, then returned.

"I, um, I got you something. From Cozumel."

Claire stared at her, an unreadable expression on her face. "You got me something?" she asked at last.

"Yes. I...I'll understand if you don't want it."

"Why wouldn't I want it?"

"Well, I didn't know if you would want a reminder of all this." She handed Claire the box. "But, here."

Claire looked at the gift in her hand. "I can't believe you bought me something." Her voice caught. "I mean after the way I treated you. Why did you even think of it?"

Abby hesitated. "Actually, it was Noah's idea. We were talking about you one day and—"

Claire's head snapped up. "Why were you talking about me?"

"Nothing bad," Abby assured her.

"No, I didn't mean it that way. I was just surprised, that's all."

"Oh. Well, I was feeling really bad about everything that had happened, and Noah suggested buying you something so you'd know I'd been thinking about you. But I wasn't sure. I didn't want you to feel like..." she trailed off, unsure how to explain. "It doesn't fix anything. It doesn't change anything. But..."

Claire shook her head. "I don't deserve this."

"Like I said, I'll understand if you don't want it."

"No, I...I'm overwhelmed." She opened the box, then touched one of the earrings with the tip of her finger. "These are beautiful. Thank you." She reached over to hug Abby.

"You're welcome."

"Jeez, we're getting maudlin here," Claire said, wiping her eyes. "We're supposed to be laughing, remember?"

Abby grinned. "Well, I did buy myself a mini conch shell with googly eyes. It's even wearing a sombrero."

For a moment Claire looked nonplussed, then she burst into laughter. "That sounds—nice."

"It's the ugliest thing you've ever seen. I don't know what I was thinking."

They laughed together.

"Thanks. I needed that."

Abby smiled. Laughing with Claire did feel good. Maybe life had a chance of getting back to normal.

After all, what else could happen?

Chapter Fifteen

The nausea that had been a part of Abby's life on and off since she'd found out she had to marry Noah had returned. This time there was a reason for it. Not a psychological one.

She looked at the two pink lines on the stick in her right hand. Not wanting to believe the outcome—maybe she'd peed on the thing wrong—she looked at the stick in her left hand. Two pink lines there too.

That made four pink lines altogether. No doubt about it. She was pregnant.

The wedding band she hadn't been able to make herself take off glinted in the light from the overhead bathroom fixture. She sighed.

So much for things going back to normal.

She tossed both sticks in the garbage, then washed her hands. Not sure what to do, she wandered downstairs into the living room, then into the kitchen. She opened the refrigerator door and stared at the contents, then closed it again. She meandered out of the kitchen and back into the living room. Finally she trudged up the stairs to her bedroom.

She grabbed Annie from the dresser, hugged her close, and sat down on the bed.

Ten minutes later, Annie was damp, and Abby still felt nauseous. Most of the time a good cry with Annie had her feeling better, but that didn't seem to be working today.

"What am I going to do, Annie? I'm going to have a baby. Noah's baby. Remember him? Noah who doesn't want to have anything to do with babies." She sighed, a big heartfelt sigh from deep in her soul. "How did this happen?"

Annie, of course, made no response. Besides, it didn't matter. Abby knew the answer. She knew how it had happened. In fact, she knew exactly how, and when, it had happened.

She reached for the dried hibiscus blossom on her nightstand and twirled the stem between her fingers.

The beach on Grand Cayman. That wonderful, erotic time on the beach, when they'd made love out in the open on the sand under the sky. The only time Noah hadn't used protection. The one time he hadn't thought about it. She hadn't either.

Until now.

And of course now it was too late. She wasn't going to tell him now. Not about that, and not about this baby. He'd made it clear how he felt about babies and commitment. Numerous times, in fact. So she knew how he would react if she told him, and she didn't want that for her baby.

She looked at the rag doll and grimaced. "I wouldn't have planned it this way, Annie. Then again, a lot of things that have happened in the last couple of months haven't been a part of any plan I ever had, that's for sure."

She'd always imagined marrying the man she loved, not getting married on television because of some game show and then falling in love with her pretend husband. And while having a baby with the man she loved sounded better than perfect, having a baby without the man she loved sounded far from it.

But that's what she was going to do. There wasn't another choice. Because the man she loved wouldn't want this baby. So she wasn't even going to tell him about it.

Ever.

Because despite everything he'd told her, Noah would want to do the right thing. It's who he was, and one of the many things she'd come to love about him in such a short time.

But because she loved him, she couldn't let him do something he would hate for the rest of his life. He would hate being tied down to her and a family. Maybe he'd even begin to hate her and the baby. She wouldn't be able to stand it if he hated their child.

She couldn't take the chance.

She dried her tears and looked around the room. What did she do now? She needed a plan.

First she needed to call her doctor. She found the number in her address book in the kitchen. She sat down at the table, then dialed with shaking fingers. "Hi, um, this is Abby Walker. I took a home pregnancy test, and it came out positive. So I was wondering what I need to do now."

"Congratulations," the nurse on the other end of the line enthused. "When was the date of your last period?"

Abby told her.

"Okay, we need to see you at about eight weeks, so let me schedule you an appointment."

Abby jotted down the date on her calendar.

"Have you been taking prenatal vitamins?"

"Well, I hadn't planned on getting, that is, this was a bit of a surprise, and I—No, I haven't been taking vitamins."

"No problem." The nurse listed several over-the-counter brands.

Abby wrote the names on a list. "Anything else I need to do or know? This is the first time I've been"—she swallowed—"pregnant."

"Other than taking those vitamins, nothing special. You'll probably be tired, so take it easy. Naps are recommended." Abby could sense the woman's smile through the phone line. "Have you experienced any morning sickness?"

"I think so. I guess I didn't realize what it was."

"Drink plenty of fluids and make sure you're eating a balanced diet. No cigarettes or alcohol."

"I don't smoke. Oh, I had a glass of champagne the other night before I knew I was pregnant. Is that going to harm the baby?"

"It shouldn't be a problem. Do you have any other questions?"

"Not at the moment."

"Don't hesitate to call if you think of something. There are plenty of good books out there that will answer most of your questions."

Abby added the titles to her list. "Great. Thank you."

"No problem. Congratulations again. We'll see you in a few weeks."

Abby clicked the phone off.

What next?

The spare room would need to be converted to a nursery. She flipped to the next page on her pad, then scribbled a list.

There. Oh, and she needed to talk to the human resources department at work to find about the maternity leave policy. She made a note in her planner.

What about daycare? Plenty of women at work used daycare providers. She'd get several recommendations before making a decision.

She looked at her lists. Although the next nine months—make that the next eighteen years—would be scary, she felt better having a plan written down in black and white.

The phone rang. She jumped.

"He-hello?"

"Abby? It's Noah."

Her gaze dropped to the lists in front of her. She gathered them into a pile, then flipped them over and placed her hand on top, as if he could see through the phone.

"Abby?"

"Oh, uh, hi. Sorry, I was just finishing something up here."

"You sound funny. Is everything okay?"

What could she say to that? "Sure, everything's fine." She hoped he couldn't hear the slight tremble in her voice.

"Good." He paused. "Listen, I finally got around to picking up those papers for us to sign. Can I bring them by today or tomorrow after work?"

Her heart plummeted to her stomach. The time had come. "Uh, sure, either day is fine. What works best for you?"

"How about tomorrow?"

"I'll be home all night after work."

"Well, I guess I'll see you tomorrow."

"Okay." She disconnected the phone, then dropped her head onto her arms on the table.

One more day and her marriage to Noah would end.

****

The doorbell pealed. Abby took a deep breath. All she had to do was get through the next ten minutes and everything would be okay. Or at least as okay as it was ever going to get.

There was no way Noah could know about the baby. He'd drop off the papers, say good-bye once and for all, and that would be that.

Then she'd be on her way to becoming a single mother. A thought that both terrified and excited her.

"You can do this." Speaking the words aloud fortified her.

She took another gulp of air into her lungs, then opened the door. She almost lost her resolve seeing him there on her doorstep. It had been more than a week since they'd attended the charity event at the television studio, and she took a moment to drink in the sight of him.

He didn't speak at first either, but stood and stared at her while she stared at him.

He broke the silence. "Hi."

"Hi." She stepped back.

"Thanks for letting me come by."

"No problem. I'm sure you want to get this taken care of as soon as possible." So did she, but for very different reasons.

"Yeah." The word sounded funny.

She couldn't put her finger on why.

"Uh, do you want to sit down?"

"Sure."

She led Noah into the living room, indicating he should sit on the couch. She trembled all over. She sank into the armchair, facing him.

"Are these the pictures from the studio?"

Her gaze followed Noah's to the coffee table, and she cursed to herself. She'd been looking at them earlier, torturing herself, and had forgotten to put them away. She'd known he was coming over. Then again, she'd had other things on her mind.

"Yes."

"May I?"

She gritted her teeth at the formality, but nodded. He flipped through the pile, the expression on his face unreadable.

He stared at one photograph. One that had been taken right after their wedding ceremony.

Finally, he set them down. "These are nice."

"Yeah.

"Are you going to keep them?"

She shrugged. She'd debated with herself so many times she wasn't sure what she'd decided. "I don't know."

"So, how have you been?"

She couldn't even begin to answer that, so she sought a safer topic of conversation. "I patched things up with Claire."

"That's great. I knew you would."

"Yeah, it's been nice talking to her again."

"Did you tell her anything? About us?"

She heard the unspoken part of the question. "I thought it would be best if she didn't know about...well, I didn't want to make things worse again by telling her... No, I didn't tell her anything. All she knows is we had to get married, and now we're getting an annulment."

Noah cleared his throat. "Right. Well, I, uh, I have the papers here. We need to sign them, and I'll have my lawyer file them."

"Okay." Her voice shook.

"We, uh, we actually weren't able to get an annulment because we, uh, consummated the marriage. So, it has to be a divorce."

Noah's words brought an ache to her chest. Relegating the intimacy they'd shared to such a technical term sent a wave of pain washing over her. At the same time she was horrified by the thought of him discussing such things with his lawyer—a stranger. How had it even come up?

On another level she noted that Noah was having trouble getting words out. He never stuttered.

Might as well get it over with. Kind of like that band-aid thing. Of course, once the band-aid came off, it exposed an open wound, but she refused to dwell on that.

"Okay, let's do it."

Noah looked at her, another unreadable expression on his face. Finally he nodded. "I've already signed them. All you need to do is put your signature by the Xs."

Her fingers shook as she took the pen he offered,

then scribbled her name in the places indicated. The shaky signature bore little resemblance to her usual, precise penmanship.

How ironic. The whole situation had started with her signing her name to something she hadn't read over carefully, and it was ending by her signing her name to something she didn't want to read over carefully.

"There. I guess that does it." She folded the papers until only the blue backing showed.

Noah took them from her. "Yeah, I guess it does. I'll make sure you get copies of these."

She nodded and crossed her arms, hugging herself.

They stared at one another. Unable to bear it a moment longer, Abby looked away. "Would you like something to drink?"

"No, thanks." Noah rose from the sofa. "I should be going."

She stood as well, her knees wobbly. She followed him to the door. He had his hand on the knob when he turned.

"This doesn't seem right."

"What?"

"Divorcing you."

Her heart halted, then started again after a long, painful moment. "Wh...what do you mean?"

Noah ran his fingers through his hair. "I don't know. All I know is this doesn't seem right. I think we have something good here." His eyes sought hers once again, and for a moment she allowed herself to get lost in their deep, blue depths.

The emotion in his eyes tore at her heart. She longed to confess her love and have him take her in his arms and never let go.

"Are you saying you want to stay married?" A flicker of hope flared in her soul.

"No." His quick denial squelched the tiny flame.

"But the thought of not seeing you again..." His voice trailed off. "We have fun together."

Her heart sank. For Noah it all came down to fun. Nothing serious. No commitments. No strings.

She had to be strong. For the sake of her baby. "It's what we decided. It's for the best." The words weren't a lie. Divorcing Noah was best. For him. And for the child she carried.

"Is it?"

"Yes. This whole thing was a game, remember?" Could he hear the sound of her heart breaking?

Some of the light faded from his eyes. "How can I forget?"

She didn't have an answer, even had Noah expected one. If she couldn't forget, how could she tell him how to do it?

He continued, "At the end, those last few days, it didn't feel like a game." The intimate tone of his voice whispered over her.

She looked away. "Don't."

"Why not?" Noah took a step closer.

She took an involuntary one back. If he got near her, if he touched her...

"Don't you remember those last few days, Abby? That was no game. It was real."

She closed her eyes, as if by doing so she could block the words from her mind. Images of their time together played against her closed lids, reminding her how real it had been. Their wedding day. The first time they'd made love. The beach on Grand Cayman. She could almost feel the warmth of the sun on her skin, the strength of Noah's body against her own. She could almost taste his kiss.

She opened her eyes to erase the images. "It's over, Noah. This is what we decided," she repeated.

"I know, I know. But now... Maybe we can see each other again sometime. Get together from time to time. To talk."

She shook her head. "I don't think that's a good idea. I think it's best we let it go." They couldn't see each other ever again. Not if she wanted to keep her secret.

"I know that's what we said, but it's different now. We're not strangers anymore."

She looked away, unable to bear the look in his eyes any longer. She wasn't strong enough to do this. Her gaze came to rest on a picture on the shelf by the TV. She and Claire at some festival.

Thoughts tangled in her mind, and in desperation she blurted, "Claire's pregnant."

Noah went very still.

She'd never know what made her say those words to him, but the look on his face gave her all the answers to the questions she'd never dared to ask. The shock etched into the lines of his face told it all. He wanted nothing to do with a baby.

"What?" The word came out hoarse. "She told you that? She said it was mine?"

She didn't answer, but hugged herself along with the tiny being inside of her, protecting it from the utter devastation on its father's face. She was doing the right thing. Noah couldn't ever know about the life she carried, even if he had helped to create it.

"That's not possible," he said, almost to himself. "What exactly did she tell you?"

"I really don't want to talk about this. I think it's best if you go." She had to get him out of her house before she broke down and cried.

"Abby, you don't understand. I—" Noah began.

"Please." She cut him off. "There's nothing more to say."

He looked at her, his eyes bleak. "No, I guess there isn't," he said at last. He turned and walked out her door.

Only then did she give in to her tears.

****

Noah sat in his car outside Abby's house. What she had told him was impossible. Claire couldn't be pregnant. Not with his baby.

Abby had said Claire had been upset about everything that had happened. She'd been angry enough to accuse Abby of purposefully manipulating the whole situation. The game show. The marriage.

But what did she hope to gain by lying about being pregnant?

He needed answers, and he wanted them fast.

He started the car and pulled away from the curb, turning at the corner and heading back toward the city. He had to talk to Claire.

In record time he reached her apartment. She looked surprised to see him. "Noah. What are you doing here?"

He ignored the question. "May I come in?"

"Sure." Still looking puzzled, Claire stepped back, allowing him in.

He gazed around the room he'd been in only a couple of times before. Although nicely decorated he couldn't help compare the modern furniture and fixtures to Abby's comfortable, somewhat old-fashioned house.

A home for growing old in with someone you cared about.

He pushed the thought aside.

He looked over at Claire, who watched him with a wary expression on her face. Had she guessed he'd discovered her lie?

She and Abby were so different. Both women were beautiful, but Claire's blue eyes didn't seem to see deep into his soul the way Abby's vivid green gaze did. And the blonde curls framing Claire's heart-shaped face didn't entice him to thread his fingers through the strands the way Abby's wavy, auburn locks did. He inhaled, as if smelling their sweet fragrance.

"Noah?"

Claire's words brought him out of his reverie. He shook his head.

"What are you doing here?" she asked again.

"I need to talk to you."

"Okay. Do you want to sit down?"

"No, thanks." He turned to pace the length of the room before looking back at her. "Did you tell Abby you were pregnant?"

"What?"

The shocked look on Claire's face was more than enough answer. She hadn't lied to him. Abby had.

An ache blossomed in his chest.

"She told you I was pregnant?"

He nodded, and Claire sank onto a chair. "Why would she do that?"

"I don't know. I was hoping you could tell me."

Claire looked stunned. Her wide, uncomprehending eyes met his. "I don't understand."

He sat on the couch, facing her. "I don't either." He paused. "I know you and Abby haven't been getting along very well lately, because of the game show and everything."

Claire looked away, but then met his gaze again. "It was hard at first, you two getting married and all."

"It wasn't real." He ignored the very real memory of Abby's body moving beneath his. He pushed away the thought of how her hand felt tucked inside his own as they strolled on the beach.

"I know, but I'll admit, I was angry with Abby for a while."

"It wasn't her fault."

"I was jealous, but I got over it. It *wasn't* Abby's fault. We talked, and I thought we were okay now." She stopped. "This doesn't make any sense. I still don't understand why she would say that. What brought something like that up? What's going on between you two?"

He evaded Claire's question. "I brought the divorce papers over to her place, and we signed them, but—" Noah paused. How much should he reveal to Claire?

"But?"

What the hell? He'd go for broke. Abby hadn't wanted to tell Claire the whole story about what had happened on their trip, and he'd respect that. But that didn't mean he couldn't tell Claire how he felt. "It didn't seem right. I asked her if we could see each other again. She said it wasn't a good idea, and when I pushed, she told me you were pregnant."

"What did you say?"

"Nothing. She wouldn't let me say anything. She asked me to leave. So, since I wasn't getting any answers from her, I decided to come here."

"And I don't have any answers for you either."

"Nope. Back to square one, I guess."

Claire looked at him, her brow furrowed. "Didn't she know you'd come here to ask me about it? She'd have to know I'd tell you it wasn't true. *You* know it couldn't be true."

He lifted his hands in a helpless gesture. He didn't have answers to his own questions, let alone Claire's.

"What are you going to do?"

"I don't know." No lie there. He didn't know what to do about Abby. He couldn't stop thinking about her. But now, even more than that, he wouldn't stop thinking about why she had lied to him.

It didn't make any sense.

Chapter Sixteen

"Did you tell Noah I was pregnant?"

Abby nearly dropped the dish she was drying.

Claire had come over, and the two friends had finished a round of cookie baking, which for Abby had been a fabulously normal thing to do in the midst of the chaos that had become her life. It had been so wonderful to talk and laugh with Claire. Things felt right again.

Until she'd asked her question. Out of the blue.

She turned to face Claire. "What?" How had she found out? Unless, Noah had—

"Noah came over."

"H...he did?" Abby didn't know what to say.

"Well, what did you expect if you tell him something like that?"

Abby sank down in a chair. "Did he ask you to marry him?"

Claire gave her a strange look. "What? Why would he do that?"

"Why wouldn't he do that? Noah would want to do the right thing. Even if he hated it."

Claire sat down across from Abby and took her hand. "Abby, what's going on? You're not making any sense."

Abby shook her head. How could she explain? Had Noah walked out on Claire, knowing she was going to have his baby? Maybe he wouldn't do something he hated after all. She didn't know if the thought made her feel better or worse.

Claire was still looking at her with a strange expression on her face.

"Wh...what did you tell him?" Abby had trouble getting the words out.

Her friend looked at her in amazement. "I didn't have to tell him anything. It's not true."

"Did you tell him that?"

"I didn't have to," Claire repeated. "It's impossible. Abby, Noah and I never slept together."

"What?"

"We'd gone out exactly three times. What kind of girl do you think I am?" Claire's tone teased, but she still looked perplexed.

Deep down inside a very secret place in her heart, Abby felt a selfish sense of relief. She'd assumed after getting to know Noah that Claire's relationship with him had been a physical one. After all, hers with him had been, and she'd known him for less time than Claire had.

"I'm sorry," she said in response to Claire's question.

Claire narrowed her eyes. "Did *he* tell you we slept together?"

"No, of course not." Even if he and Claire had been lovers, Noah never would have talked about it.

"Then why in the world would you tell him I was pregnant?"

"I wanted to see how he'd react."

"Abby, honey, I'm still not following you."

Abby stood to pace around the kitchen. How could she explain any of this to Claire? She couldn't explain it to herself. She stopped at the window, staring out, but not really seeing into the yard beyond.

"I learned a lot about Noah while we were on that trip together. One of the things I learned was that he didn't want to have children. Ever." Saying the words hurt, and she folded her arms, hugging herself.

"So you wanted to torture him a little by telling

him I was pregnant?"

"No, no, I didn't want to hurt him." Could she trust Claire with the truth? How would she react? She'd been so angry about Noah and Abby getting married, wouldn't knowing about this make it worse? Abby didn't think she could go through that again.

But it would be so nice to confide in someone. She took a deep breath, but didn't turn from the window. "Claire, I'm pregnant."

When Claire made no response, Abby looked over her shoulder. Claire's open mouth formed a small *O*.

"I'm sorry," Abby whispered again.

Claire shook her head. She blinked. "You and Noah?" The words sounded strangled.

Abby nodded.

Silence fell. The clock over the sink ticked loudly in the stillness. A myriad of emotions crossed Claire's face. Finally she met Abby's gaze again. "Wow."

"Yeah." She paused. "Do you understand now?"

Claire rose, coming to stand in front of Abby. "No, I don't understand. Why did you tell him *I* was pregnant?"

"Because I wanted to see what he would do. As much as Noah doesn't want to have children, he's a good man, and he would want to do the right thing. Even if it was the wrong thing for him. And I couldn't let him do that."

"He has the right to know about his baby."

Abby shook her head. "No. I can't tell him. Don't you see? He'd want to stay married for the sake of the baby. I wouldn't be able to stand what that would do to him. And what it would eventually do to the baby."

"I don't think you're giving him enough credit. Maybe you don't know him as well as you think."

Claire's tone was soft, her eyes compassionate.

"He told me. Over and over. I *do* know him, and I'm telling you I'm right about this." Tears filled Abby's eyes, then spilled over onto her cheeks.

Claire moved to embrace her. "Shhh, okay." She stroked Abby's hair as she hugged her.

Abby allowed her friend to comfort her, then pulled away. She wiped her eyes and tried a half-hearted smile. "Thanks. I'm a mess. Hormones."

Claire leaned back against the counter. "What are you going to do?"

"I'm going to have this baby."

"And you're not going to tell Noah?"

"No." Abby's voice trembled, but her resolve remained firm. "Promise me you won't tell him either."

"I would never do that."

Abby sighed. "I know. I'm so scared he's going to find out."

Claire turned to walk around the kitchen. Her gaze came to rest on a photograph sticking out from beneath some papers on the desk next to the refrigerator. She moved the paper aside, then picked up the stack of wedding and honeymoon pictures. She flipped through them.

Abby held her breath and watched Claire to see her reaction, but her face didn't reveal her thoughts. She'd taken the news about how real Abby and Noah's honeymoon had been better than Abby had expected. But in the back of her mind, she wondered how much Claire could handle. Would looking at the pictures of the wedding be too much? Would she snap again? And would Abby blame her if she did?

When Claire came to the last photograph, she gazed at it before setting the whole stack back on the desk. She turned to Abby. "You guys look great together."

"What?"

"You and Noah. You make a great couple." The words held no hint of anger.

Abby hid her surprise and waved her hand. "That was all for show. We had to pretend."

Claire shook her head. "This isn't pretending." She tapped the pile of pictures. "Do you love him?"

Abby didn't want to lie to her friend. Weren't they past all that now? Especially since Claire knew the truth about Abby's relationship with Noah.

But it was hard to say the words aloud, to admit them to someone else. "Does it matter?" she asked instead.

"You tell me." She grabbed Abby's left hand. "You didn't take off your wedding ring."

Abby remained silent, not sure how to respond.

Claire didn't push her, but looked at her with sympathetic and sad eyes. "You can divorce Noah, and you can choose to not tell him about the baby, but for the record, I think you're making a mistake."

****

That night as Abby lay in bed, Claire's words played over and over in her mind.

Did Noah deserve to know about his child? Probably.

But Abby was so scared. She loved the tiny being inside of her already and didn't wish for anything to hurt it. Ever.

And telling Noah about their baby was setting them up for a world of hurt. He already hurt so much from the guilt he carried around. Abby didn't want to be responsible for adding more to the burden.

And besides, she and the baby would be fine on their own. They would have a roof over their head, and Abby had a secure job. True, she wouldn't be able to stay home with the baby full time as she might have wished, but she'd be able to pay the bills and provide. The essentials were covered.

And she'd love the baby more than enough to make up for the fact that her child wouldn't have a father. Plenty of kids were raised by one parent these days. She wouldn't be the only one doing it.

And although she didn't relish telling her parents, once they'd adjusted to the circumstances, they would be thrilled to have a grandchild.

And who knows, maybe someday she'd find someone who would love her and the baby, and they'd become a family. Noah would be more than happy to have some other man raising his baby, so he wouldn't need to worry about it. No strings attached, he'd said.

And that decided it. She wouldn't tell him. Their paths wouldn't cross again. They'd signed the divorce papers. There was no reason for them to see each other again.

It didn't matter that a part of her would always love him. He didn't love her. Besides, their lives were on different tracks. He'd be off on his adventures.

She had a different kind of adventure stretching before her. One that he wouldn't want to be any part of.

The thought made her heart ache, but she took comfort in the fact that she'd always have a little piece of him in the life they'd created together. She'd have to be satisfied with that.

****

"Are you okay, dear? You don't seem yourself today." His mother's voice broke into Noah's reverie.

He half smiled at the words. A familiar warmth washed over him at her being able to discern his mood. Which is why he'd driven to Indiana.

Running his fingers through his hair, he sighed. He hadn't felt like himself in a long time. How could he explain that to the woman looking over at him so expectantly? He couldn't explain it himself.

"I don't know, Mom."

"Talk to me, Noah." She sat down on the arm of the couch.

He turned to pace the length of the basement, passing the Foosball table he and his brothers had spent countless hours at while they were growing up. He barely noticed the assortment of photographs on the walls, but he knew every picture by heart and could almost name the dates of each of the Christmases, holidays, and family celebrations chronicled there. Over the years the family had grown, and more and more smiling faces mugged for the camera.

Finally he turned to face his patiently waiting mother.

What could he say to her? That he thought he might be in love, but he wasn't sure what that felt like, so what if he wasn't? He could say that, but if it didn't sound right in his head, he doubted the words would come out any more clearly.

One of the pictures caught his eye again, and, out of the blue, words Abby had spoken that day in Grand Cayman came back to him. "May I ask you something?"

"Of course."

"If you had to choose between traveling around the world and having the whole family together, what would you pick?"

His mother sent him a reproachful look.

"I know, I know. Stupid question." He paused. "Tell me this. Do you ever feel like you missed out on things? Because of me?" He held his breath, waiting for her answer.

She rose, coming to stand before him. "What on earth are you talking about, 'because of you'?"

"Well, you know. Having to get married and all. Because you were pregnant. With me." He couldn't meet her gaze.

"Had to get married?"

"Yeah, you know. Because of me."

"Noah, dear, I'm not sure what this is all about, but your father and I didn't *have* to get married, we wanted to. From the moment I met him, I knew he was the man for me. We didn't *have* to do anything."

Her words didn't convince him. He'd carried his guilt with him for so many years, he couldn't let it go as easily as that. "But you could have been an artist or—"

"The only thing I wanted to be was Ed's wife. And the mother of his children." She reached up to lay a soft hand against his cheek. "We were thrilled when we found out we were going to have you. How could you think anything else?"

He cursed to himself at the tears that sprang to her eyes. He gathered her to him in a comforting hug. He hadn't meant to hurt her. Inhaling, he breathed in the familiar floral scent of the perfume she always wore. It brought back countless memories of being comforted as she held him in her arms. Now he was the one who held her. "I'm sorry, Mom. Please don't cry."

After a moment, she pulled away, dabbing at her eyes with the hem of her apron. "Have you always felt like this?"

No use pulling punches now. "For a long time. As long as I can remember," he admitted.

"Oh, Noah." Her voice was anguished. "Why didn't you ever talk to us about this? Why didn't you tell us how you felt?"

He shrugged. "I don't know. I figured if I could bring pieces of the world back to you from my travels, you wouldn't feel like you were missing out on so much. I guess I didn't think there was anything to talk about."

"Well, now that's the most ridiculous thing I've ever heard. Your father and I haven't missed out on anything. Other than maybe having you around more."

He flinched at the slight note of recrimination in her voice, but he deserved it. Abby sure had hit the nail on the head with that one. How had she picked up on it so quickly, when he had missed it all these years?

He shook his head and smiled to himself. Because she was Abby, that's why.

"What are you smiling about?" His mother asked, interrupting his thoughts.

Noah didn't answer her question. Instead, he asked one of his own. "So, this is what you've always wanted? What you have now?"

"Absolutely." There was no hesitation in her voice.

Noah shook his head and offered a rueful smile. "I've been an idiot, haven't I?"

"Yes." The word held an equal combination of frustration and affection. Then with that natural instinct all mothers seem to have, she asked, "Is that why you never thought about settling down yourself?"

He nodded again. "Uh, yeah. I didn't want to be tied down and stuck in one spot like you were. Like I thought you were," he amended.

"Oh really, Noah." Now that the tears were gone, he could hear the exasperation in her voice.

"I know, I know," he said again. He had no defense. Looking back now, it all did seem a little ridiculous. But he'd carried the guilt with him for so long, it was a part of him.

His mother laid a soft hand on his arm. "Why don't you stay here for a couple of days. Your father and I would love to have you."

"I wish I could, Mom, but I'm leaving tomorrow on a trip."

"Where to this time?"

"Central America. There's a festival in Panama."

"Well, I'm sure you'll have fun, dear."

Noah smiled at the word. It brought back an avalanche of memories. "I suppose."

"Promise me something?"

"Anything."

"While you're gone, think about what we talked about."

"I will." More than she knew.

****

Noah arrived in Panama the next day. A cab took him to his hotel. Outside the open window, palm trees rushed by on the side of the road. The balmy breeze ruffled his hair. The air smelled salty. An endless stretch of sand met the sea in the distance.

He raised his camera to his eye and snapped a dozen pictures. Then he sighed. He could take all the pictures he wanted, but although Panama was a beautiful country, for some reason the sky didn't seem as blue as it should. And the backdrop of sand and sea seemed less vivid, as if something were missing.

Abby.

Panama didn't have Abby.

He waited in line to check in at his hotel. The clerk handed him his room key. Noah turned from the desk. A woman with long brown hair that curled around her shoulders stood a few feet away with her back to him.

"Abby?" Her name slipped out before he could stop it.

The woman turned. Brown eyes surveyed him from between lashes coated with thick mascara. Her glance slid down his body, then met his again. "No, but I could be." The throaty purr reeked of suggestion.

"No, thanks. Uh, sorry, I thought you were

someone else."

The woman's eyes reflected her disappointment. "Well, maybe some other time." She sauntered away.

Noah didn't bother to watch her go. He double checked the room number on his keycard, picked up his duffel bag, and headed toward the elevators.

Upstairs, he tossed the bag on a nearby chair. The king-sized bed in the middle of the room brought a smile to his lips. Abby had been so freaked out the first night of their cruise. But then they'd spent two amazing nights in that same bed.

His body stirred at the vivid memory. He hadn't been with another woman since meeting her. He collapsed on the bed and laced his fingers beneath his head.

He missed her.

But the physical ache of wanting her didn't come close to the emotional ache that grew in his heart each day he spent without her.

The conversation he'd had with his mother right before he'd left came to mind. About the guilt he'd carried for so long and the reasons for it. Was he ready to let it go?

Could he give Abby what she'd always wanted? A home, a family? Was he ready to commit?

And if he was, would she want those things with him?

Since they'd signed the divorce papers and she'd lied to him about Claire, he hadn't seen her or talked to her. He'd called a couple of times, but she hadn't picked up the phone. And if she was that desperate to avoid him, he didn't think showing up at her house unannounced was a good idea.

Although he needed answers, he wanted to give her time, before he confronted her again.

He sighed and looked at the clock on the bedside table. Too early to turn in for the night. Might as well go down to the bar for a bite to eat.

Downstairs he passed by several empty tables in the restaurant and grabbed a seat at the bar. He ordered a burger and fries, then turned to survey the room while he waited. A group of women at a corner booth tried to catch his eye, but he ignored them. He ate a few pretzels while he waited for his food.

A few moments later the bartender placed a frozen margarita on the bar in front of him.

He looked up. "I didn't order this."

The bartender jutted out his chin. "From the ladies."

Noah glanced over his shoulder. The trio of women waggled their fingers at him. He raised the glass. "Thanks," he mouthed. He turned back to the bar.

"Hey." Someone slid onto the stool next to his.

He looked over. One of the ladies from the corner booth. He bit back a sigh. "Hey," he responded.

Wide blue eyes studied him with open appreciation. Long, blonde hair hung straight down her back. "I'm Theresa."

"Noah." He turned his attention back to the pretzels. Maybe she'd take the hint.

"So, Noah, are you here on business or pleasure?"

In the past, his response would have been an immediate *both*. His business brought him pleasure. But on this trip, the pleasure part seemed to be missing.

The blonde waited for an answer, an expectant smile on her face.

"Business."

"My girlfriends and I," she waved toward the back of the restaurant, "came down for the festival. Have you had the chance to see any of it, or has your business kept you busy?" She laughed at her own joke.

He fought the urge to roll his eyes. "Yeah, I've seen some of it."

"Isn't it amazing?"

"Sure. Look—" He fumbled for her name. Six weeks ago, he would have had her room number already. Tonight he couldn't wait to get rid of her.

"Theresa," the girl supplied.

"Sorry. Look, Theresa, thanks again for the drink." He nodded at the frosty concoction and rose from his stool. "But I have to get going."

Disappointment flooded her eyes. "Are you sure you don't want to join us for a little while?"

The bartender brought Noah's burger and fries. "Can I grab that to go?" He tossed some bills down on the bar, then turned to the blonde. "Sorry, I have an early flight tomorrow," he lied. "And I need to give my wife a call before I turn in." The words slipped out before he'd even realized he was going to say them.

"Oh." Her face fell at this news. "Well, okay, then. It was nice meeting you, Noah."

"Yeah, you too." He grabbed his food from the bartender. "Thanks." He strode from the room without a backward glance.

What he wouldn't give for his words to be true. He wanted to call his wife. Abby. And tell her he was on his way home. He wanted to tell her how much he missed her and how he couldn't wait to see her.

Realization hit him with the force of a hurricane.

He *was* ready to commit.

Now the question remained, was Abby?

Chapter Seventeen

"Will your husband be joining us?"

Abby's heart stalled in her chest. She looked up at the nurse hovering over her. "Um, no. Not today." Not ever.

Did she even have a husband anymore? Noah must have filed the papers by now.

"No problem," the other woman assured her. "If he has any questions, let him know he can call anytime."

Abby nodded. The lump in her throat made speech impossible.

"Okay, dear, the ultrasound tech will be in here in a moment."

"Thank you," Abby managed.

The door closed with a click. She looked around the small, sterile room. Suddenly, she felt very alone.

Claire had offered to come with her to her appointment, but Abby had refused. Things were back to normal with Claire, but Abby didn't want to push her.

And part of her was feeling very selfish. She was going to see her baby for the first time today. She didn't want to share the moment with anyone.

Well, there was one person she'd like to share it with, but that wasn't going to happen.

A soft knock on the door interrupted her thoughts. The technician poked her head through the opening. "Are you all set in here?"

"Yes."

"Great." The woman pushed Abby's dressing

gown out of the way and squeezed gel onto her abdomen.

The thick liquid warmed her bare skin.

"Okay, let's take a look." She pressed a wand to Abby's stomach. She moved the device around. "There." She pointed to the monitor close to Abby's head. "That's your baby."

Tears rolled unchecked down Abby's cheeks as she watched the tiny image on the screen. It flicked rapidly.

"Is...is that the heartbeat?" Awe tinged her soft whisper.

"Yep. Amazing isn't it? The wonder of life is truly a miracle." She tapped on the keys below the monitor. "I'll print this out for you." The machine whirred and a long strip of black and white paper poured from a slot in the side.

"Here you go." She handed it to Abby. "Your first baby pictures."

"Thank you," Abby stammered.

The technician grinned. "This is the best part of my job." She nodded toward the paper in Abby's hand. "After you show that to your husband, you can hang it on the fridge."

Abby ignored the stab of the words as the technician switched off the monitor, then wiped Abby's stomach with a damp cloth. "Right now it probably doesn't look like much, but we'll do several more sets as you progress along. Next time it will actually look like a baby. You'll be amazed how much it grows each time."

Abby stared at the blurry image. She had a baby with a heartbeat.

She couldn't imagine anything more amazing than that.

"Okay, we're all set here. Why don't you get dressed, and the doctor will be back in a few minutes to finish up."

Abby divested herself of the hospital gown and redressed in her own clothes. She sat on the edge of the examining table and swung her legs while she waited for the doctor to return.

She'd tucked the ultrasound picture into her purse, but in her mind's eye she kept seeing the tiny image. Her heart swelled with love for her unborn child.

"Hi, Abby.

She jumped at the sound of the doctor's voice. She hadn't heard the door open.

"Sorry, didn't mean to startle you."

"No, I was just lost in thought."

The doctor checked the chart. "Everything looks great. You're right on schedule. Keep taking your vitamins and," she nodded toward the water bottle in Abby's hand, "drink plenty of water. Did you have any questions?"

"Should I limit my activities in any way?"

"Well, I wouldn't go cliff diving, get on a rollercoaster, or take up skydiving. Normal activities are fine. Exercise is recommended. We offer some great prenatal classes through the hospital." She handed Abby a pamphlet. "Walking every day is good too. Just don't overdo anything. If you're tired, rest. Oh, and intercourse is definitely okay."

Abby choked on the sip of water she'd taken. "What?"

The doctor smiled. "The husbands are usually curious about that one. Intercourse during pregnancy is perfectly safe for the baby. As long as you don't experience any discomfort, you can enjoy sex right up to your final weeks. Just go with the old adage, 'if it feels good, keep on doing it, if it doesn't, stop'".

Abby's face flamed. "Right." She didn't bother telling the doctor that particular activity wouldn't be a problem. Or an option for that matter.

****

The light on the answering machine blinked at Noah when he walked into his apartment. The flight home and subsequent cab ride from the airport had seemed interminably long. Never before had he been so glad to be home.

Had Abby called while he'd been gone? His heart beat a little faster. He pressed the 'play' button.

"Hey, Noah, where've you been?" John's voice filtered from the machine. "Neumann and I are getting together at Al's Saturday afternoon if you're in town. Hope you can make it."

The machine shifted to the next message.

"Hi, Noah, dear. Everyone's coming over for dinner Saturday night. Hopefully you'll be back. Love you," his mother signed off.

No Abby. A wave of disappointment washed over him.

He grabbed the phone and dialed her number. They needed to talk.

The phone rang four times before her machine picked up. He hung up without leaving a message.

He glanced at his watch. He'd have time to swing by the bar before heading to Indiana.

****

"What the hell is that on your finger?"

Noah frowned. Then he noticed the direction of Neumann's gaze. He looked down at his hand, wrapped around his beer bottle. He still wore his wedding ring. He hadn't even remembered he had it on. When Abby had first placed it on his finger, it had felt uncomfortable and out of place. Now wearing it felt so natural, he didn't even notice it any more. It had become a part of him.

Like Abby was a part of him.

He didn't have time to dwell on the warm feeling the thought brought, because his buddies were still staring at his finger, identical looks of shock contorting their faces. He grinned at their comical expressions.

"I got married." He took a sip of beer and tried to look nonchalant. Instead of the usual shudder of fear, the words brought a sense of warmth and rightness. An image of Abby formed in his mind.

His wife.

"What?"

"What the—?"

The words chorused around him as his friends stared with open-mouthed astonishment.

"You what?"

"I got married," he repeated. "Didn't I tell you guys?" Of course he hadn't told them, but it couldn't hurt to have a little fun with this. The last few days had been anything but.

"Okay, smart ass. What's going on?" John demanded.

"Yeah, are you kidding us, or what?" Neumann added.

"I'm not kidding, guys. Look, it was kind of a spur of the moment thing."

"You got married? For real?" John sounded skeptical.

Noah half smiled at that. How often had he and Abby declared their marriage wasn't for real? "Yeah, for real." He hadn't been able to bring himself to file the divorce papers yet, so technically and legally they *were* still married.

"Who is this girl?"

"Her name's Abby."

"And?" Neumann probed.

"That's it."

"That's it? That's all you're going to tell us?"

"Yep." He stood, fished in his back pocket for his wallet, and tossed some bills down on the bar. "I have to go."

"Where the hell do you think you're going?"

"Big family dinner." He looked at his watch. "I'm supposed to be in Indiana in an hour."

"You can't leave now."

Noah headed for the door, then looked back over his shoulder. "I have to. I'm already late. Mom won't keep dinner waiting too long."

He strolled out of the bar, whistling a jaunty tune. A grin crossed his face as he recalled the unbelieving expressions on his friends' faces when he'd told them about Abby. Man, he wished he'd had his camera.

Then he sobered. How would things work out with Abby? Would she ever talk to him again? Explaining to his friends that he wasn't married anymore would not be fun.

For a lot of reasons he didn't want to contemplate. The biggest one being that the thought of not being married to Abby made it feel like someone had punched a huge hole in his chest.

He needed to talk to her. And soon.

It turned out he was the first to arrive at his parents' house, but only by a minute or two. His brothers and sisters along with their broods came piling into the house, and for a moment familiar chaos reigned as hugs and kisses were delivered all around. Everyone oohed and aahed over Erin, the latest addition to the family.

Then his mom turned to speculating who would be next.

"Not us," Eric said, his tone adamant.

"Yep, sorry, Mom, we're done," Angela agreed, patting her husband's arm in a reassuring manner.

"We are too," Tom jumped in, casting a meaningful look at Barbie.

"We'll see," she teased with a mischievous smile.

Everyone laughed, then the girls went into the kitchen to help his mother with dinner preparations, and the guys settled into the well-worn couches in the living room with his dad to keep an eye on the kids, who played on the floor in front of them.

After a while Fiona toddled over and climbed up onto his lap. "Hi, Unca No." She snuggled into him and twirled the spout of hair her ponytail made on top of her head.

"Hey, sweetie."

As he cuddled her close, he watched his other nieces. What would it feel like to have a child of his own laughing with delight as Meg and Zoe were doing now as they watched the antics of their younger siblings? A child that was his and Abby's. Maybe they'd have a boy, the first grandson among all of the granddaughters. What would it be like knowing that Abby was helping in the kitchen with the rest of the girls, laughing and talking with his mom as they worked?

He was so lost in his daydream it took him a moment to realize someone was calling his name.

"Noah!"

"What?" His attention snapped to his mother, who had come into the room without him noticing. She had a strange look on her face.

"I called you three times."

He shook his head to clear it. "I'm sorry...did you need something?"

"Yes, dear. I need that big bowl of your grandmother's for the salad. I think it's on one of those high shelves in the basement."

He rose, displacing Fiona, who scurried to rejoin her cousins on the floor. "I'll get it for you."

"I'll come down with you. I'm not sure which box it's in." Margaret Grant looked toward the kitchen. "Barbie, if I'm not back in five minutes, stir that big pot on the stove, would you?" Not waiting for an answer, she motioned Noah to proceed her down the stairs.

Once downstairs, his mother turned to him.

"So, did you give any thought to what we talked about last time you were here?"

He smiled. Trust his mother to cut right to the chase. "I did."

"And?"

"And you had it right all along. I should have talked to you about it a long time ago."

"So why were you finally willing to talk about it now?"

"Abby."

"Abby?" A spark of interest lit her eyes.

"Yeah. Mom, you're gonna love her."

She threw her arms around him and hugged him. "If you do, I'm sure I will." She paused. "So, where did you meet this girl?"

He laughed. "You wouldn't believe me if I told you."

"Try me."

He told her the whole story. "So, now I have to convince her I want to stay married."

His mother stared at him, a bemused look on her face.

"What?"

She shook her head. "I can't believe you're married." Tears filled her eyes.

He hugged her again.

She pulled away and dabbed at her eyes. "I wish we could have been there."

"So do I, but we have pictures and a DVD."

"Well, of course I'll want to see the pictures, but don't forget we'll want to see the two of you often as well." The tone of her voice provided a gentle reminder of their previous conversation.

"Don't worry, I won't forget."

She stood on tiptoe to kiss his cheek. "I'm so proud of you, Noah. When do we get to meet her?"

"As soon as I can convince her how much I love her. Any suggestions?" His mother had provided a lifetime of love to her family. If anyone could figure out a way to help him with Abby, she could.

"Just tell her what's in your heart."

He nodded. "Do you mind if I don't stay for dinner?"

She laughed. "I can honestly say, this is one time I don't mind at all."

Upstairs, he said good-bye to his brothers and sisters. "Sorry I can't stay. I need to take care of some things." He needed to convince Abby that they were meant to be together, and he had an idea of how to get started.

He was ready to commit. To be married for real in every sense of the word and all it entailed. 'Til death do us part.

For a moment, he looked at everyone gathered around the dinner table. Another image of Abby and him surrounded by their own children came to mind, and he imagined them being a part of family dinners like this one. He could see her clear as day, feeding small morsels of food to their little one, like Michelle did for Alli.

"Noah, you look like you've seen a ghost." Angela came into the room, breaking into his reverie. She placed a steaming dish on the table.

"Yeah." He smiled. "The ghost of Christmas future."

****

It seemed corny and clichéd, but he'd done it anyway. Noah stood on Abby's porch clutching a bouquet of roses in one hand. A nervous flutter filled his stomach. A new sensation for him. Never before had he felt so unsure about what to say to a woman.

Of course, never before had it been so important to say the right thing. He'd never asked a woman to stay married to him.

Would she believe him when he told her how he felt?

After all, he'd spent their entire cruise telling her how much he didn't want to have anything to do with what he was about to propose.

He'd believed it. But he hadn't counted on Abby turning his whole world topsy-turvy. He hadn't counted on falling in love with her.

But how did she feel about him? Only one way to find out.

He checked the box he'd placed outside the door one last time, patted the papers tucked inside his jacket pocket, and took a deep breath. He reached out to press the doorbell, then had to close his fingers into a tight fist to stop them from shaking. He pulled one more breath into his lungs, uncurled his fist, and rang the bell.

Chapter Eighteen

Abby groaned at the sound of the doorbell. The pizza guy was early. He'd said more than an hour.

She'd filled the bathtub with a mound full of bubbles, and they floated on top of the warm water. She left the lavender-scented bathroom and made her way into the living room, tightening the sash of her robe.

She peeked through the window, but the frost-covered glass obscured anything more than the shadowy outline of the figure on her porch. She opened the door as far as the chain would allow and peered through the slit.

"Hi."

Her breath caught in her throat. What was Noah doing here? She fought the urge to glance down. Would he be able to tell she was pregnant? She pushed the thought away. She still had many weeks to go before she started showing.

"May I come in?" he asked when she didn't say anything.

She hesitated. "I don't think that's a good idea." What if she slipped up and said something? It had been hard enough seeing him once before and keeping her secret.

"Please." His soft voice matched his earnest expression. He thrust out the flowers he clutched in one hand. "These are for you."

She almost smiled. She would bet good money that he'd never gotten flowers for a woman before.

"Please," he said again. "It's important."

She wavered, curious about why he was there.

She unchained the door and opened it all the way, then stepped back to allow him in. A gust of cold air followed him into the living room, and she shivered. She closed the door before turning to face him.

"It's still cold out there." Noah held out the roses once again.

She took them, bringing the bouquet up to her face to inhale their sweet fragrance. But she wouldn't give in to the romantic gesture. "I'm sure you're not here to talk about the weather."

He smiled. "No." He stepped toward her. "I've missed you." He raised a hand to touch the side of her face.

She closed her eyes. "Please, we've been through this."

"No, we haven't."

"What?" Her eyes opened and locked onto the deep blue of his, the expression in them intense as he studied her.

"*You've* been through this. *You* decided there wasn't anything between us. But you're wrong." He captured her face between his palms. He lowered his head, at the same time raising hers. "There's everything between us." He whispered the words, then claimed her mouth in a soul-shattering kiss.

Helpless to do otherwise, she kissed him back, forgetting all the reasons she shouldn't. It felt so right to be back in his arms. The familiar pressure of his lips stroking over hers threatened to drown her in the bittersweetness of it all.

Before she could pull away, he broke the kiss. Again, he searched her eyes with his own. His question, when it came, was unexpected. "Why did you tell me Claire was pregnant? Why did you lie to me?"

She lowered her eyes and quelled the urge to wrap her arms around her abdomen. She couldn't answer that.

"Well, it doesn't matter."

Her gaze flew to his.

"I'm sure by now Claire's told you it's not true?"

Abby nodded.

"And did she tell you why it couldn't possibly be true?"

Unable to find her voice, she nodded again. Why was Noah bringing this up now? Why did it matter?

"Good. Because having a baby with Claire wouldn't fit into my plans."

Her heart froze. The ache spread until her whole body felt numb. She couldn't bear to hear him talk about how much he never wanted to have children. She'd heard it a hundred times before. She heard it every night in her dreams. Her shattered dreams.

"I think it would be pretty hard to explain to people if your husband were having a baby with your best friend."

Her head jerked up. The flowers fell from her listless fingers. "Wh...what are you talking about?"

Noah smiled. "Do you want to hear about my plans, Abby?"

"Your plans?"

"Oh yes, I have big plans for the future. Our future."

Their future?

He must have read the question in her eyes. "That's right. Can I tell you about my plans? You're in them, by the way," he added. "In fact, you are them."

Noah had plans? For the future? With her? A thousand questions peppered her mind, and she shook her head to clear them, her thoughts impossibly tangled.

"I thought we'd start with the fence. You know, the white picket one you always wanted?" He fished in the inside pocket of his leather jacket and pulled out a sheaf of papers. He held them out to her.

She took them, but stared with unseeing eyes. He'd ordered a fence? It seemed like forever ago she'd told him of her dreams for the future. She couldn't believe he'd remembered. A tiny flame of hope flickered to life inside her heart.

"They can't come for another thirty days, so we'll have to keep the dog on a leash until then."

"The...the dog?" Abby found her voice at last.

"Yeah." Noah turned and vanished out the front door. He returned a second later with a box in his arms. "I hope you like her. Isn't she adorable?"

Dumbfounded, she peered into the box. A tiny black Labrador puppy nestled on top of an old cotton T-shirt. She reached in to pet the dog gently, not wanting to disturb its sleep. She raised uncomprehending eyes to Noah.

"What—?" She stopped, then cleared her throat and tried again. "Why—?" She got no further.

Noah set the box down, then dropped to one knee in front of her.

Her mouth fell open.

He took her left hand and ran his thumb over her wedding band. "You didn't take this off." Noah's voice was soft, his eyes mesmerizing as he gazed up at her.

She could only shake her head, once again unable to form a sound around the lump in her throat.

"We never did this right, you know." He smiled. "Abby, I love you."

Her heart hummed at the confession.

"Will you stay married to me?"

Was she dreaming? Was this really Noah kneeling in front of her saying such wonderful things? How could this be the same man who had told her that he didn't want anything to do with getting married? Ever.

He somehow read her thoughts again, because

he smiled. "I'm not the man you think I am. Hell, I'm not the man I thought I was."

"You...you're not making any sense."

"Actually, it's all making perfect sense now. Finally. Don't you see it? *We* make perfect sense. You and me. Together."

"We do?"

Noah rose. He placed a tender kiss on her lips. A haze of tears blurred her vision, and she blinked to clear it. Noah wiped the moisture off of her cheek with the pad of his thumb.

"I've been so stupid. I mean, here I've been trying to convince myself, and everyone else, that I wasn't like the rest of my family. I wanted to be alone and on my own, and as it turns out I couldn't have been more wrong."

"You couldn't?"

"Abby, all I can think about is being with you. Being married to you. For real." He smiled, then continued, "As in *'til death us do part* and everything that goes with it."

She wanted nothing more than to collapse in his arms and confess her own love. But more was at stake here now than her happiness. The things Noah said were wonderful. She had dreamed about hearing them, but did he mean them?

"What about your job? Can you live without your adventures?"

Noah laughed. "Honey, I have the feeling that being with you is going to be all the adventure I'll ever need." He paused. "I can't say I won't travel. It's what I do, and I love my job." He kissed her forehead. "Would you be upset if I still traveled?"

"I wouldn't like it if you were gone all the time, but I know how much you love your job. I wouldn't want you to give it up for me."

"You can go with me when I travel."

She shook her head. "I can't go with you."

"Come on, Abby. We had a great time on our honeymoon. Just think, we could do that all the time. If you're worried about money, don't be. I make enough to—"

"No, it's not that."

"Then what is it?"

"There's something you need to know. Something that might change your mind about all of this."

"Whatever it is, it doesn't matter. I'm laying my heart on the line here. Nothing is going to change my mind about wanting to be with you. I want to carry on the Grant tradition and make lots of babies with you and stay in this house with you forever."

She caught her breath. "Wait. Say that again."

"I could live here with you forever."

"No, the part before that. The part about the babies."

Noah laughed and gathered her into his arms. He kissed her upturned lips. "I think we should start with three, and then see what happens from there."

She hugged him close for a moment longer before she pulled away. Another tear slipped down her cheek as she gazed up at him. Her heart wobbled. She swallowed to ease the dryness in her throat. The time had come to tell him. How would he react? The love shining in his eyes gave her courage. "What would you say if I told you we've started already?"

She held her breath. Noah's response would seal her fate one way or another. Saying he wanted children and being faced with the reality were two different things. How did he really feel?

His brow furrowed. "What are you talking about?"

She took a deep breath. "Noah, I'm pregnant."

Silence met her words.

She risked a glance at him. He stood rigid. Pain

clutched her heart. She looked away from his shock-filled eyes.

"What?" The word came out hoarse.

She hugged herself.

"How—" he stopped. "How did it happen? I mean, we were, I was, always so careful."

"Grand Cayman," she whispered. She turned away. She couldn't bear to look at him anymore. She went to stand in front of the window. Tears rolled unchecked down her face.

The silence stretched until she couldn't stand it anymore.

"Look," she said. "I don't expect anything from you. I won't ask you for anything, and I—" Warm hands on her shoulders stopped her words.

"Look at me."

She shook her head.

"Abby." He turned her shoulders so she had no choice but to face him. He tilted her chin up with his forefinger. "What do you mean, you don't expect anything from me?"

"Please." Her voice trembled. Her legs felt like they might not support her. "It's okay. I understand. You can go. I won't contact you. I wasn't going to tell you, but—"

"You weren't going to tell me what?" He sounded rough, almost dangerous.

"I...I wasn't going to tell you I was pregnant."

"You weren't going to tell me about my baby?" The calm in his voice sounded forced.

She shivered. "I know how you feel about having children, and I want you to know that you don't have to worry about it. This baby won't be a burden to you."

"A burden?"

"I'm sorry." Her voice cracked. "I didn't plan this. I know you don't want kids, so I—"

"So you jumped to the wrong conclusion. Again."

His loving tone belied the sting of the words.

"Wh-what?" The words surprised her almost as much as the tender note in his voice.

"Didn't you hear a word I said over there?" He motioned toward the front door, an indulgent smile on his face. "I *want* to have a family with you."

"I know that's what you said, but I'm sure you didn't expect it to be so soon."

"No, I didn't, but that doesn't matter." He looked at her. "Are you under the impression that I'm upset?"

She frowned. "You seemed so shocked when I told you."

"I won't lie to you. I *was* shocked. How did you feel when you found out?"

A half smile quirked her lips. "Shocked."

"See? You took me completely by surprise, but that doesn't mean I'm unhappy about it. I think it's wonderful."

"Are you sure? I mean, Noah, this is your life. Your entire life will be different."

"I know." His thumbs stroked over her face, wiping away the tears. "Isn't it wonderful? We're going to be together. We're going to have a family." A touch of awe tinged the words.

"Are you sure?"

"Oh, yes, I'm sure." The look in his eyes put her fears to rest once and for all.

She sighed. The tension left her body. "I love you, Noah."

He exhaled. "It's about time you said that," he teased. "I love you too, Abby Grant." He kissed her. Long. Deep. Sealing his vow.

Then he drew her close once again. She cuddled against his strength. She'd found everything she'd ever wanted in the arms of this man. Her wild wedding weekend had turned into the best thing that had ever happened to her. Noah had come into her life and turned it upside down.

She wouldn't want it any other way. She couldn't wait to continue the adventure her life with him would surely be.

His gaze dropped to her middle, and his hand curved over her stomach. He dropped to his knees and buried his face in the folds of her robe.

She threaded her fingers through his hair, pressing him closer.

His head moved from side to side, loosening the sash at her waist. He separated the sides of her robe, reaching in to span her waist with his hands. He pressed a kiss to her abdomen.

She shuddered at the feel of his mouth on her bare skin. Desire raced through her. Heat spread, making her limbs feel heavy.

"Noah." She sighed his name. It had been forever since he'd touched her.

He caught the longing in her voice immediately. "Can we?"

"The doctor said it was fine."

His head jerked up, his surprised gaze meeting hers. "You asked? Who were you planning on—"

"No one," she interrupted. She smoothed the frown line between his eyes with her fingers. "The doctor offered way more information than I needed to know."

He stood and scooped her into his arms. "Now I don't know about that. I bet all of that information might just come in handy."

She curled into him. "Upstairs. Bedroom at the end of the hallway." She nuzzled his neck, then trailed her lips over his jaw, around to his ear. She nibbled on the lobe.

"We'll never make it upstairs if you keep that up."

"Promises, promises."

He took the stairs two at a time. In the bedroom,

he tumbled her onto the bed. He shrugged out of his jacket, then yanked his shirt over his head. The hurried movements betrayed his impatience.

The sight of his naked chest sent a spiraling wave of heat to her very core. She reached out to him. A moan escaped from her throat.

"Patience, love, I'm hurrying." He shimmied out of his pants. Finally, he joined her on the bed. He eased the robe from her shoulders, baring her flesh to his hungry gaze. His hand cupped her breast.

"Fuller," he murmured before dipping his head to suckle her.

She pulled him closer, exalting when his arms wrapped around her, holding her close to the heat of his naked body.

With another low moan, she surrendered to him.

****

Later, snuggled against his chest, she slid her leg over his, entwining their limbs. His fingers feathered down her arm and back up. Goose bumps followed in the wake of his light touch.

She'd just decided she could stay in his arms that way forever, when the doorbell rang.

Noah's hand stilled. "Expecting someone?"

"Pizza," she murmured, then made a low sound of protest in her throat when he moved away from her. "Where are you going?"

He untangled himself from her embrace. "To get the pizza." He slid into his jeans.

"I'm not hungry anymore."

The sound of his laughter lingered as he headed downstairs.

While he was gone, Abby grabbed his T-shirt from the floor and slipped it over her head. His spicy scent enveloped her.

In a moment, he returned, the pizza box in one hand, two sodas in the other. "I hope you don't mind," he held up the cans, "I raided your fridge."

"Of course not. It's your house now too," she added shyly.

He looked pleased. "Yeah, I suppose it is."

Abby arranged the pillows behind her and leaned back. Noah sat down on the foot of the bed and folded his legs beneath him. He placed the open pizza box between them.

The smell of tomatoes, gooey cheese, and oregano made her stomach growl.

He grinned. "Not hungry, hey?"

She made a face at him. "Well, I am eating for two." She marveled at how easy it was to joke with him about the baby, when for the longest time she'd vowed to keep it a secret from him. Had been so afraid he'd find out.

"Any cravings?"

"Not really." She took another bite of pizza. "I am hungry a lot, though."

"Good." He handed her another slice. "Keep eating. We want him to be big and strong."

Abby stopped with the piece of pizza halfway to her mouth. "Him?"

Noah swallowed, then nodded. "I have a theory." His eyes sparkled. He looked genuinely excited.

"Already? That was fast." Part of her mind still spun at Noah's ready acceptance of her news.

"Not really. I've had this theory for a couple of days."

She choked on the sip of soda she'd taken. "What? But you just found out—"

He looked into her eyes. "Abby, I told you. I came here today to convince you that I wanted to spend the rest of my life with you. Raise a family with you." He smiled. "Little did I know you were already ahead of me. Which reminds me," he dug his wallet out of his back pocket, "I guess I won't be needing these anymore." He tossed a handful of square packets onto the bedspread.

Abby laughed. "No, I guess not."

His eyes turned serious as he gazed at her once again. "You must have cast a spell on me. I didn't even think about this on Grand Cayman." He leaned in to kiss her. "You've given me everything I've always wanted. Actually," he corrected, "you've given me everything I never knew I wanted, but now I know I can't live without." His fingers trailed down her cheek. "Thank you."

His hand moved to her abdomen. He stroked the spot for a moment, almost as if caressing the life growing inside her.

"So when does this little guy make an appearance?"

Tears blurred her eyes at the combination of love and awe in his tone. She had to clear her throat to answer. "October."

"October," he repeated. He shoved the empty pizza box out of the way and drew her into his arms. He kissed the top of her head. "A honeymoon baby." His voice held a note of deep satisfaction. Then his chuckle vibrated through her. "Now that's what I call carrying on the Grant tradition."

A word about the author...

Debra St. John has been reading and writing romance since high school. She always dreamed about publishing a romance novel some day. *Wild Wedding Weekend* is her second book; her first was *This Time for Always*.

Debra lives in a suburb of Chicago with her husband, who is her real life hero. She is past president of her local RWA chapter and has also served in the capacity of advisor, manuscript chair, and secretary.

Visit her at her website,
www.debrastjohnromance.com.
Or check out her posts on Sundays at the Acme Author's Link, http://acmeauthorslink.blogspot.com.

Thank you for purchasing
this Wild Rose Press publication.
For other wonderful stories of romance,
please visit our on-line bookstore at
www.thewildrosepress.com

For questions or more information
contact us at
info@thewildrosepress.com

The Wild Rose Press
www.TheWildRosePress.com